新
民
说

成
为
更
好
的
人

BOB
DYLAN
THE LYRICS 1961—2012
鲍勃·迪伦诗歌集

"爱与偷"

[美]鲍勃·迪伦 著

罗池 陈震 李皖 译

广西师范大学出版社
·桂林·

AI YU TOU

LYRICS: 1961-2012
Copyright © 2016, Bob Dylan
All rights reserved.
著作权合同登记号桂图登字：20-2017-053 号

图书在版编目（CIP）数据

鲍勃·迪伦诗歌集：1961—2012. "爱与偷"：汉
英对照／（美）鲍勃·迪伦著；罗池，陈震，李皖译.
桂林：广西师范大学出版社，2017.6（2018.7 重印）
　书名原文：LYRICS: 1961-2012
　ISBN 978-7-5495-9691-1

　Ⅰ. ①鲍… Ⅱ. ①鲍…②罗…③陈…④李…
Ⅲ. ①诗集－美国－现代－汉、英 Ⅳ. ①I712.25

中国版本图书馆 CIP 数据核字（2017）第 079139 号

出　　版：广西师范大学出版社
　　　　　广西桂林市五里店路 9 号　邮政编码：541004
网　　址：http://www.bbtpress.com
出版人：张艺兵
发　　行：广西师范大学出版社
　　　　　电话：（0773）2802178
印　　刷：山东临沂新华印刷物流集团有限责任公司印刷
　　　　　山东临沂高新技术产业开发区新华路
　　　　　邮政编码：276017
开　　本：740 mm×1 092 mm　1/32
印　　张：8.875　　字数：95 千字
版　　次：2017 年 6 月第 1 版　　2018 年 7 月第 3 次
定　　价：25.00 元

如发现印装质量问题，影响阅读，请与出版社发行部门联系调换。

目 录

"爱与偷"

附加歌词

摩登时代

共度此生

暴风雨

The St. Regis
CLUB

Bye & Bye — By — Breathen Come Syle

1. From moment I'm at with you is a moment — despair —
A Lithonia girl in the world won you ~ cruel conspire
Bye & Bye I'm ~~breathing breakin simple~~ lookg for a blud in my eye

2. Painty the fence / Spreadly Rouben Mind /
Gonn establish my rule by civil wars,
Paint my stove/ if you got thing to show up n round

3. Negotin day Heaven Forces on dis plan —
Gotta be quick on trigger — preserve a lot
You hear how if people gon help you n out — ⑤

   Bridge: I etc Czour my inituals on every noodes behind
   The only tiny bit I ode to me is the how i mind

4. Mix George — Dont you ~~honey~~ manamanor — but you Shet
   Might know Baby — For Gods sake, ~~Craby~~ you see
   How you think it'd work if I dch you still gonn slop pee in
   Dont be ~~loony~~ Dont be gloom ... we gon a / Sit our heads togethr & make our plans to come
   — He's in a rage — still we gonna set out — stab stand in the field

5. Miss Beth / Loyon on this couch —
   He got this curious drown / Arrees fallignand
   with my poems to Come your mind
   low down single man —
   Low down snm gol' hair
   Aw Heer stab ya when ya stand —

   Bridge: Thing doing the honeycomb boogie out on the northend of town
   I etc at night in the words you cant hear a sound

6. Payen Gonna Mad / Mizzin the feelin bent
   Smokestack Lightin' skratch' teh gold
   In gratitude just makes my blood run cold
   restless tho, ~~feel~~ Letty it go ... 100 miles
   breakin i'm doing for me, but;
   all i kno too slow -

   You promised me darlin'
   The day but we last
   that yesterdays woud crumble
   Oh how you forget -

"爱与偷"
"Love and Theft"

罗池　译

　　《"爱与偷"》是鲍勃·迪伦的第三十一张专辑，2001年9月11日正式发行时，恰逢"9·11"恐袭。部分歌词在收入本书时有改动，《走过青山绿岭》《等着你》二首为本书追加。

　　专辑名出自美国文化史家埃里克·洛特（Eric Lott）1993年的著作《爱与偷：黑面歌舞团和美国工人阶级》（*Love & Theft: Blackface Minstrelsy and the American Working Class*），指美国主流文化一面歧视黑人，一面又通过戏仿和挪用来"偷窃"黑人的歌舞和文化，实际上是迷恋黑人的健康肉体，表明了一种深爱。这个专辑大量引用、"偷窃"了美国传统民谣（尤其是密西西比三角洲蓝调）的元素，向前辈们致敬：歌名都出自传统民谣的经典主题，曲子则用另一首老歌的旋律重新编配，歌词里充满美国民谣史上的金句妙语。另外，歌中还有多处穿插了日本当代作家佐贺纯一的黑帮小说《浅草博徒一代》英译本（*Confessions of a Yakuza*）中的句子，连原作者都表示荣幸。

T. S. 艾略特在《论菲利普·马辛格》(*Philip Massinger*)中有名言:"不成熟的诗人模仿,成熟的诗人偷窃,差诗人糟蹋他们获得的东西,好诗人则把它变得更好,或至少不一样。好诗人把他的赃物熔焊到整个独特的、完全不同的情感之中,差诗人则把它扔进一堆杂乱无章的东西里面。"鲍勃·迪伦也从不避讳自己对前人的大胆借鉴,他曾在 1964 年的《时代正在改变》专辑说明文字中写道:

> 对,我就是思想的窃贼,
> 哦不,我但愿是灵魂的小偷,
> 我在建造并且重建。

罗池

大宝弟大宝哥 [1]

大宝宝哥和大宝宝弟

他们耍飞刀去钉树皮

累成两包死人骨头

还埋头苦干不停不休

他们住在挪得之地 [2]

把命运交在上帝手里

他们安安静静生活下去

大宝宝哥和大宝宝弟

啊，他们要回乡下，他们要后撤

他们搭上了欲望号街车 [3]

望着橱窗里的核桃派

很多东西他们喜欢但从来不买

---

1. 歌名源自同名英国传统童谣："大宝哥和大宝弟／商量好要干一仗／因大宝哥说大宝弟／弄坏了他的鼓拨浪。／这时飞来只大老鸹，／黑得跟柏油桶一般；／两个英雄都吓怕，／浑忘了他们的争端。"刘易斯·卡罗尔在《爱丽丝镜中奇遇记》第四章写到这对互相争斗的兄弟。

2. 挪得之地，意即流放地，见《旧约·创世记》4:16，该隐因杀其弟而被上帝放逐，"去住在伊甸东边挪得之地"。注释凡涉《圣经》处，译文一律引自和合本，供大致的参照；《圣经》中屡见者，一般仅引一条。

3. 指涉美国剧作家田纳西·威廉斯的戏剧《欲望号街车》。

两人都不是转身就跑
他们远行以太阳为目标
"主人的声音在召唤我。"
大宝宝哥对大宝宝弟说

大宝宝弟和大宝宝哥
除了这些还有故事更多
他们走在宏伟的树林里
他们知晓那微风中的秘密
大宝宝哥对大宝宝弟说
"你的一举一动惹恼了我。"
像两个宝宝在一个妈妈怀里
大宝宝哥和大宝宝弟

啊，他们生活甜甜蜜蜜
大宝宝哥和大宝宝弟
他们总是差一点点就成功
他们拿到游行的批准还有警察护送
大宝宝弟——他跪下来四脚着地
说："给我扔点啥吧，先生，求求你。"
"对你好的东西对我也不错。"
大宝宝哥对大宝宝弟说

啊童年的梦想是不死的欲望

有一条崇高真理是神圣的教纲

他们姿态很低他们总抓住时候

他们似乎决定一直往前走

一个是个卑贱又可怜的老汉

另一个会把你戳死在你的地盘

"我为你的公司已经付出太多。"

大宝宝哥对大宝宝弟说

Tweedle Dee & Tweedle Dum

Tweedle-dee Dum and Tweedle-dee Dee
They're throwing knives into the tree
Two big bags of dead man's bones
Got their noses to the grindstones
Living in the Land of Nod
Trustin' their fate to the hands of God
They pass by so silently
Tweedle-dee Dum and Tweedle-dee Dee

Well, they're going to the country, they're gonna retire
They're taking a street car named Desire
Looking in the window at the pecan pie
Lot of things they'd like they would never buy
Neither one gonna turn and run
They're making a voyage to the sun
"His Master's voice is calling me,"
Says Tweedle-dee Dum to Tweedle-dee Dee

Tweedle-dee Dee and Tweedle-dee Dum
All that and more and then some
They walk among the stately trees
They know the secrets of the breeze
Tweedle-dee Dum says to Tweedle-dee Dee
"Your presence is obnoxious to me."
They're like babies sittin' on a woman's knee
Tweedle-dee Dum and Tweedle-dee Dee

Well, they're living in a happy harmony
Tweedle-dee Dum and Tweedle-dee Dee

They're one day older and a dollar short
They've got a parade permit and a police escort
Tweedle-dee Dee—he's on his hands and his knees
Saying, "Throw me somethin', Mister, please."
"What's good for you is good for me,"
Says Tweedle-dee Dum to Tweedle-dee Dee

Well a childish dream is a deathless need
And a noble truth is a sacred creed
They're lying low and they're makin' hay
They seem determined to go all the way
One is a lowdown, sorry old man
The other will stab you where you stand
"I've had too much of your company,"
Says Tweedle-dee Dum to Tweedle-dee Dee

密西西比

我们走的每一步都按着定数

你的日子我的日子都有限度

时间越堆越高，我们争斗我们煎熬

我们都拘禁其中，没有出路可逃

都市就是丛林，好多游戏可以玩

在市中心落入了陷阱，才迷途思返

我在乡下长大，后来为工作进了城

刚放下行李我就被烦恼缠上了身

什么都无法给你，我从来一无所有

就连给我自己也总是空空的两手

天空火焰弥漫，痛苦倾盆倒落

你的东西我都买不起，不如下次再说

我的思维和表达能力都那么高超

却根本说不清你真是莫名其妙

只有一件事我犯了大错

待在密西西比整日蹉跎

啊，魔鬼进了街巷，骡子进了厩舍 [1]

---

1. 被别家的骡子钻进自家的厩舍，在美国俚语中是被戴绿帽子的意思。

你随便说点啥吧，我全都听在耳

我想起罗茜答应过的誓言

我梦见我睡在罗茜的枕边 [1]

走在飘落满地的枯叶中间

感觉像个陌生人没有谁待见

好多事情我们永远都无法化解

我知道你很抱歉，我也一样抱歉

有人会向你伸出援手有人却无动于衷

昨晚我还认识你，今晚我却不懂

我需要用些强大的东西来让自己分心

我要一直看着你直到我双目失明

啊我追随南天星来到这里

我渡过大河只为了和你在一起

只有一件事我犯了大错

待在密西西比整日蹉跎

啊我的船已碎成碎片然后转眼沉底

我在毒药中淹溺，没有未来，没有过去

但我的心却不知疲惫，它轻盈它自由

我一无所获，除了感激那些人曾与我同舟

---

1. 指涉美国传统民谣《罗茜》(Rosie)，罗茜是帕奇曼农场黑人囚歌中理想的女性形象。

人人都在奔忙，即便早已到了地方

人人都要奔去某一个方向

与我同行吧宝贝，总之跟我一起

那么生活就会开始变得有趣

我的衣服湿漉漉，紧贴在我的身体

但不像我把自己困在一个墙角那样的紧逼

我知道我的幸运是你行善的结果

那就把你的手给我吧，说你愿属于我

啊，空虚无穷无尽，黏土一样凉透

你随时可以回头，但你不能从原路往回走

只有一件事我犯了大错

待在密西西比整日蹉跎

Mississippi

Every step of the way we walk the line
Your days are numbered, so are mine
Time is pilin' up, we struggle and we scrape
We're all boxed in, nowhere to escape
City's just a jungle, more games to play
Trapped in the heart of it, trying to get away
I was raised in the country, I been workin' in the town
I been in trouble ever since I set my suitcase down
Got nothing for you, I had nothing before
Don't even have anything for myself anymore
Sky full of fire, pain pourin' down
Nothing you can sell me, I'll see you around
All my powers of expression and thoughts so sublime
Could never do you justice in reason or rhyme
Only one thing I did wrong
Stayed in Mississippi a day too long

Well, the devil's in the alley, mule's in the stall
Say anything you wanna, I have heard it all
I was thinkin' about the things that Rosie said
I was dreaming I was sleeping in Rosie's bed
Walking through the leaves, falling from the trees
Feeling like a stranger nobody sees
So many things that we never will undo
I know you're sorry, I'm sorry too
Some people will offer you their hand and some won't
Last night I knew you, tonight I don't
I need somethin' strong to distract my mind
I'm gonna look at you 'til my eyes go blind

Well I got here following the southern star
I crossed that river just to be where you are
Only one thing I did wrong
Stayed in Mississippi a day too long

Well my ship's been split to splinters and it's sinking fast
I'm drownin' in the poison, got no future, got no past
But my heart is not weary, it's light and it's free
I've got nothin' but affection for all those who've sailed with me
Everybody movin' if they ain't already there
Everybody got to move somewhere
Stick with me baby, stick with me anyhow
Things should start to get interesting right about now
My clothes are wet, tight on my skin
Not as tight as the corner that I painted myself in
I know that fortune is waitin' to be kind
So give me your hand and say you'll be mine
Well, the emptiness is endless, cold as the clay
You can always come back, but you can't come back all the
    way
Only one thing I did wrong
Stayed in Mississippi a day too long

夏日

夏日、夏夜已成过去
那些夏日和夏夜都已成过去
我知道一个地方那里的故事还在继续

我盖房子在山坡，我在泥滩养猪猡
我盖了房子在山坡，我在泥滩里养了群猪猡
我讨了一个长发美女，她来自高贵的印第安部落

各就位预备——举起酒杯大声唱
各就位预备举起了酒杯大声唱
啊，我站在桌面上，我提议这一杯敬祝大王

啊，我开着一辆凯迪拉克爆胎漏气
姑娘们都说："你这个大明星早已过气。"
我的荷包满满，每一毛钱花光都不心疼
既然你明知那人一直是我但你怎能说你爱的是别人？

啊，大雾迷蒙你无法看清陆地
大雾迷迷蒙蒙让你无法看清陆地
但你到底有什么用，如果你连个老商人都经受不起？

婚礼的钟声敲响，歌队开始吟唱
唉，婚礼的钟声敲响了歌队已开始吟唱
白天看着好好的，到晚上就全不一样

她望着我的眼睛，她握紧我的手
她望着我的眼睛，她握紧我的手
她说："你不能够重回过去。"我说："不能够？你说什么，
  你不能够？你当然能够。"

你从哪里来？你要去往哪里？
对不起，你不需要知道这些东西
啊，我的脊背在墙上靠得太久，就像已经被粘牢
为什么你不把我的心再伤一次就当是个好运道

我有八个化油器，小子，全被我启动
啊，我有八个化油器呢小子，全被我启动
我的汽油不够了，我的发动机开始要罢工

我的狗狗都在吠，肯定有人来了附近
我的狗狗都在吠，肯定有人来了附近
我把锤头抡得当当响，小美人，但钉子就是没动静

如果你有话，就大声讲否则保持沉默

啊，如果你有话，现在就大声讲否则保持沉默
如果你想要打探消息你可以找警察跟你说

政界人士已穿上他的慢跑鞋
他肯定是奔向事务所，一刻不停歇
你从那宽宏慷慨的天才榨取血汗
你的眼睛滴溜溜转——你当我是个笨蛋

站在上帝的河边，我的灵魂开始战栗
站在上帝的河边，我的灵魂开始战栗
我就指望你了亲爱的，让我喘一口气

啊，只等乌云消散我一早就要上路
唉，只等乌云消散然后我一早就要上路
真想暴跳如雷——放一把大火就当分手礼物

夏日、夏夜已成过去
夏日、夏夜已成过去
我知道一个地方那里的故事还在继续

Summer Days

Summer days, summer nights are gone
Summer days and the summer nights are gone
I know a place where there's still somethin' going on

I got a house on a hill, I got hogs all out in the mud
I got a house on a hill, I got hogs out lying in the mud
Got a long haired woman, she got royal Indian blood

Everybody get ready—lift up your glasses and sing
Everybody get ready to lift up your glasses and sing
Well, I'm standin' on the table, I'm proposing a toast to the
    King

Well, I'm drivin' in the flats in a Cadillac car
The girls all say, "You're a worn out star."
My pockets are loaded and I'm spending every dime
How can you say you love someone else when you know it's
    me all the time?

Well, the fog's so thick you can't spy the land
The fog is so thick that you can't even spy the land
What good are you anyway, if you can't stand up to some
    old business man?

Wedding bells ringin', the choir is beginning to sing
Yes, the wedding bells are ringing and the choir is beginning
    to sing
What looks good in the day, at night is another thing

She's looking into my eyes, she's holding my hand
She's looking into my eyes, she's holding my hand
She says, "You can't repeat the past." I say, "You can't?
   What do you mean, you can't? Of course you can."

Where do you come from? Where do you go?
Sorry that's nothin' you would need to know
Well, my back has been to the wall for so long, it seems like
   it's stuck
Why don't you break my heart one more time just for good
   luck

I got eight carburetors, boys, I'm using 'em all
Well, I got eight carburetors and boys, I'm using 'em all
I'm short on gas, my motor's starting to stall

My dogs are barking, there must be someone around
My dogs are barking, there must be someone around
I got my hammer ringin', pretty baby, but the nails ain't
   goin' down

You got something to say, speak or hold your peace
Well, you got something to say, speak now or hold your
   peace
If it's information you want you can go get it from the
   police

Politician got on his jogging shoes
He must be running for office, got no time to lose
You been suckin' the blood out of the genius of generosity
You been rolling your eyes—you been teasing me

Standing by God's river, my soul is beginnin' to shake

Standing by God's river, my soul is beginnin' to shake
I'm countin' on you love, to give me a break

Well, I'm leaving in the morning as soon as the dark clouds
　　lift
Yes, I'm leaving in the morning just as soon as the dark
　　clouds lift
Gonna break in the roof—set fire to the place as a parting
　　gift

Summer days, summer nights are gone
Summer days, summer nights are gone
I know a place where there's still somethin' going on

掰了掰 [1]

掰了掰，我还发出恋人的感慨
坐在手表上我就能准时合拍 [2]
用甜腻腻的韵脚我把情歌唱起来
掰了掰，对你我要瞟一个大眼白

我满城狂欢——甩着舞伴团团转
我知道谁能依靠，我知道谁能信服
我在观察道路，我在研究尘土
我满城狂欢，跳完我的最后一圈

啊，穿越荆棘我踉踉跄跄我跌跌撞撞
只为了那个人她是我一心的渴望

我轻轻摇曳——我用尽了所知的一切
我对自己说我找到了真正的幸福
我还有一个梦想未曾被人辜负

----

1. 原文"bye and bye"，又可作"by and by"，是美国传统民谣主题，可指
不久将来、美好的未来、生离死别、后世在天堂重聚等，表达祈愿、悼亡、诀别。
2. 准时合拍，字面意为"在时间上"。

我轻轻摇曳，去到红玫瑰疯长的旷野

啊，未来对我而言已经是一个过去
你曾是我的初恋然后你将成为我的结局

爸爸发了疯，妈妈，她的心好痛
我要发动内战来建立我的统治
从深深的海底筑起万仞千尺
我要送你上高空去看那烈火熊熊

Bye and Bye

Bye and bye, I'm breathin' a lover's sigh
I'm sittin' on my watch so I can be on time
I'm singin' love's praises with sugar-coated rhyme
Bye and bye, on you I'm casting my eye

I'm paintin' the town—swinging my partner around
I know who I can depend on, I know who to trust
I'm watchin' the roads, I'm studying the dust
I'm paintin' the town making my last go-round

Well, I'm slippin' and slidin', walkin' on briars
To get to the one that my heart desires

I'm rollin' slow—I'm doing all I know
I'm tellin' myself I found true happiness
That I've still got a dream that hasn't been repossessed
I'm rollin' slow, goin' where the wild red roses grow

Well the future for me is already a thing of the past
You were my first love and you will be my last

Papa gone mad, mama, she's feeling sad
I'll establish my rule through civil war
Bring it on up from the ocean's floor
I'll take you higher just so you can see the fire

寂寞的一天蓝调

啊，今天已经成了孤单寂寞的一天
呀，今天已经成了孤单寂寞的一天
我坐在这儿胡思乱想
我的心思飞到十万八千里远

啊，他们跳交叉曳步舞，把沙子撒在地板
他们跳交叉曳步舞，他们把沙子撒在地板
当我离开我多年的女友
她就站在大门槛

啊，我爸早就死了，我哥哥去当兵送了命
啊，我爸早就死了，我哥哥去当兵送了命
我姐姐，她离家出走嫁人了
后来再也没有音讯

萨曼莎·布朗[1]有四五个月住在我的屋子
萨曼莎·布朗有四五个月住在我的屋子

---

1. 萨曼莎·布朗（Samantha Brown，1970— ），美国电视旅游节目主持人，实地介绍全世界的度假胜地、酒店、山庄、民宿等。

我不懂别人会怎么看
反正我没跟她睡过一次

道路塌方——天气不适合人类或兽类
哈，道路塌方——天气不适合人类或兽类
真好笑，你最难以割舍的那些东西
就是你最不需要的累赘

我离磨坊还有四十英里——我推到超速挡
我离磨坊还有四十英里——我推到超速挡
给我的电台设定频道
我告诉自己我还活在世上

我看到你的老情人来了——走过荒郊野地
我看到你的老情人来了——走过荒郊野地
他根本不是一个绅士——他烂到骨子里
他是个懦夫他还偷东西

啊我的船长他仪表堂堂——他学识渊博他样样在行
我的船长，他仪表堂堂——他学识渊博他样样在行
他不会多愁善感——他根本不操心
有多少同伙要被送葬

昨夜里风声低吟，我使劲想要听清

昨夜里风声低吟——我使劲想要听清

我告诉自己有事情要发生

但根本就没有动静

我要宽恕失败者——我要给群众演说

我要宽恕失败者，小子，我要去给群众演说

我要去给被征服者教导和平

我要驯化那些骄傲的家伙

啊树叶在林中窸窣——东西从搁架上掉落

树叶在林中窸窣——东西从搁架上掉落

你会需要我的帮助，小心肝

单靠你自己你连爱都不能做

Lonesome Day Blues

Well, today has been a sad ol' lonesome day
Yeah, today has been a sad ol' lonesome day
I'm just sittin' here thinking
With my mind a million miles away

Well, they're doing the double shuffle, throwin' sand on the
    floor
They're doing the double shuffle, they're throwin' sand on
    the floor
When I left my long-time darlin'
She was standing in the door

Well, my pa he died and left me, my brother got killed in
    the war
Well, my pa he died and left me, my brother got killed in
    the war
My sister, she ran off and got married
Never was heard of any more

Samantha Brown lived in my house for about four or five
    months
Samantha Brown lived in my house for about four or five
    months
Don't know how it looked to other people
I never slept with her even once

The road's washed out—weather not fit for man or beast
Yeah, the road's washed out—weather not fit for man or
    beast

Funny how the things you have the hardest time parting with
Are the things you need the least

I'm forty miles from the mill—I'm droppin' it into overdrive
I'm forty miles from the mill—I'm droppin' it into overdrive
Got my dial set on the radio
I'm telling myself I'm still alive

I see your lover-man comin'—comin' 'cross the barren field
I see your lover-man comin'—comin' 'cross the barren field
He's not a gentleman at all—he's rotten to the core
He's a coward and he steals

Well my captain he's decorated—he's well schooled and he's skilled
My captain, he's decorated—he's well schooled and he's skilled
He's not sentimental—don't bother him at all
How many of his pals have been killed

Last night the wind was whisperin', I was trying to make out what it was
Last night the wind was whisperin' somethin'—I was trying to make out what it was
I tell myself something's comin'
But it never does

I'm gonna spare the defeated—I'm gonna speak to the crowd
I'm gonna spare the defeated, boys, I'm going to speak to the crowd

I am goin' to teach peace to the conquered
I'm gonna tame the proud

Well the leaves are rustlin' in the wood—things are fallin'
    off of the shelf
Leaves are rustlin' in the wood—things are fallin' off the
    shelf
You gonna need my help, sweetheart
You can't make love all by yourself

浮浪
（过分的要求）

在窗户的外边

阳光照得闪闪刺眼

它穿过小巷子——穿过百叶窗

又是日复一日的一天

蜜蜂嗡嗡嗡地飞

树叶与它们唱和

我爱上了我的远房表妹

我对自己说我和她在一起会永远快乐

我一直留神想听见脚步声

但我根本听不到什么

要是在船上我会钓鲶鱼

钓上很多，有时真的太多

盛夏的微风轻轻地吹

正在酝酿一场狂飚

有时我真是蠢得可笑

让自己卷入某种风潮

老头子在附近转悠，有时他们

会和年轻人把关系闹僵

但老也好小也好，年纪根本不重要

到头来还不都是一样

有个人是那位大佬的马屁精

在你意料之外他会大驾光临

想威胁你——逼迫你——想激起你的恐惧感

但这样只会适得其反

市郊有一片小树刚刚新栽

老林子早已消失不再

从前二尺六寸的大径材

剩下的树皮一直烧到现在

他们说时世艰难，如果你不信

你不妨跟着感觉一路向前

我才懒得去管——到处都时世艰难

我们只能眼看它怎样发展

我家老头，他像个封建领主

老不死的堪比九命猫

没见过他跟我妈妈争吵

不论精彩人生还是归于无聊

你还闻得到松木在燃烧

你听得见学校在打铃

要尽量坐在最靠近老师的地方

如果你想学到些真本领

罗密欧对朱丽叶说："你面容憔悴。

这样可不能让你显得青春洋溢！"

朱丽叶对罗密欧说："既然你那么在意

为什么还不赶紧远离。"

他们都想方设法离开了这里

冷雨会叫你一阵战栗

他们去了俄亥俄、坎伯兰、田纳西

剩下的那些人都躲进匪区流域[1]

如果你还敢来干涉我或阻挡我的路

你这样做就是玩儿你自己的命

我可不像表面那样宽容或冷静

我已经看惯了太多的心痛和纷争

我爷爷是捕野鸭的高手

他只需要装起套索和罗网

我奶奶会用破布缝出新的衣裳

我不知道他们有没有梦想或渴望

我觉得我倒是有过一个，那就是

———————

1. 美国南北战争时期，北军舰队占大优势，封锁南方水运并沿河而上至密西西比河等地，南军依沿岸要塞据守，后来残兵流寇退至上游，这些地方泛称"匪区流域"。

在每个圣诞前夜的圣诞颂歌里把圆圈舞跳个不停

我已经抛弃所有的梦想和渴望

在烟草里把它们埋葬

想踢开某某人并不总是轻而易举

要花些功夫——这可能是个棘手的任务

有时某人会要你放弃一些东西

不管泪流与否，都是过分的要求

Floater
(Too Much to Ask)

Down over the window
Comes the dazzling sunlit rays
Through the back alleys—through the blinds
Another one of them endless days
Honey bees are buzzin'
Leaves begin to stir
I'm in love with my second cousin
I tell myself I could be happy forever with her
I keep listenin' for footsteps
But I ain't hearing any
From the boat I fish for bullheads
I catch a lot, sometimes too many
A summer breeze is blowing
A squall is settin' in
Sometimes it's just plain stupid
To get into any kind of wind

The old men 'round here, sometimes they get
On bad terms with the younger men
But old, young, age don't carry weight
It doesn't matter in the end
One of the boss' hangers-on
Comes to call at times you least expect
Try to bully ya—strong arm you—inspire you with fear
It has the opposite effect
There's a new grove of trees on the outskirts of town
The old one is long gone

Timber two-foot six across
Burns with the bark still on
They say times are hard, if you don't believe it
You can just follow your nose
It don't bother me—times are hard everywhere
We'll just have to see how it goes

My old man, he's like some feudal lord
Got more lives than a cat
Never seen him quarrel with my mother even once
Things come alive or they fall flat
You can smell the pinewood burnin'
You can hear the school bell ring
Gotta get up near the teacher if you can
If you wanna learn anything
Romeo, he said to Juliet, "You got a poor complexion.
It doesn't give your appearance a very youthful touch!"
Juliet said back to Romeo, "Why don't you just shove off
If it bothers you so much."
They all got out of here any way they could
The cold rain can give you the shivers
They went down the Ohio, the Cumberland, the Tennessee
All the rest of them rebel rivers

If you ever try to interfere with me or cross my path again
You do so at the peril of your own life
I'm not quite as cool or forgiving as I sound
I've seen enough heartaches and strife
My grandfather was a duck trapper
He could do it with just dragnets and ropes
My grandmother could sew new dresses out of old cloth
I don't know if they had any dreams or hopes
I had 'em once though, I suppose, to go along

With all the ring dancin' Christmas carols on all of the
    Christmas Eves
I left all my dreams and hopes
Buried under tobacco leaves
It's not always easy kicking someone out
Gotta wait a while—it can be an unpleasant task
Sometimes somebody wants you to give something up
And tears or not, it's too much to ask

洪水

（献给查理·帕顿）[1]

洪水汹涌——没日没夜汹涌

所有真金白银都被洗劫一空

大乔·特纳[2]看看西看看东

从他头脑里的小黑屋

他来到了堪萨斯城

十二大街和万恩街

什么都无法站立

洪水铺天盖地

洪水汹涌，冲垮棚屋大片大片

人们失去财产——人们离开家园

伯莎·梅森[3]摇散它——砸烂它

---

1. 查理·帕顿（Charley Patton，1891—1934），美国民谣歌手，被誉为"三角洲蓝调之父"，有歌曲《洪水铺天盖地》（*High Water Everywhere*），讲述1927年密西西比河大洪水给黑人带来的痛苦。洪水、大河在迪伦此前的歌曲中也出现过多次。

2. 大乔·特纳（Big Joe Turner，1911—1985），美国密苏里州堪萨斯城的民谣歌手，人称"蓝调老大"。

3. 伯莎·梅森，夏洛蒂·勃朗特的小说《简·爱》中男主角罗切斯特的疯妻子。查理·帕顿妻子的名字也叫伯莎。

然后又把它吊在墙上

说："你要跟他们指定的人跳舞

否则你就根本不会跳舞。"

现实真是残酷

洪水铺天盖地

我饥渴地迷恋风驰电掣

一脚跨上野马福特[1]

快跳上车吧，宝贝，叫内裤飞窗外去

我会给你写诗，叫肌肉男发疯去

我可不是没戴假发的猪猡[2]

我希望你好好待我

一切分崩离析

洪水铺天盖地

洪水汹涌，高过我头顶六英寸

棺材在大街上到处乱扔

像一个个铅铸的气球[3]

---

1. "野马"是美国福特汽车公司 1964 年推出的紧凑型跑车品牌。
2. 源自英国诗人克里斯蒂娜·罗塞蒂（Christina Rossetti）的童谣《如果猪戴上假发》（If a Pig Wore a Wig）。
3. 铅气球飘不起来，常比喻毫无用处、不被别人接受、头脑昏昏等。

大水冲进维克斯堡[1]，不知道我该做点什么

"不要伸手拽我，"她说

"你没看到我也溺水了吗？"

现实真是艰苦

洪水铺天盖地

啊，乔治·刘易斯[2]告诫英国人、意大利人和犹太人

"小子，不要对随便每一种视角

都敞开你的头脑。"

在五号公路那边他们诱捕查尔斯·达尔文

法官对治安官说

"给我抓住他不论死活

随便怎样，我不在意。"

洪水铺天盖地

布谷是只小小鸟，它一边飞一边叫

我在传布上帝的福音

我在剜掉你的眼睛

---

1. 维克斯堡，美国密西西比州城市，水运枢纽，1927 年洪灾时收容了大批难民。
2. 可能指乔治·刘易斯（George Lewis，1900—1968），美国爵士乐黑管演奏家，或乔治·亨利·刘易斯（George Henry Lewes，1817—1878），英国哲学家、评论家，达尔文的支持者。

我找肥婆南希要东西吃，她说："自己去橱柜拿——
你已经长那么大了，小伙子，
但你不可能比你本人更伟大。"
我告诉她我根本不在意
洪水铺天盖地

我一大早就要起床——我相信我会掸干净扫帚
远远离开那些女人
我跟她们保持大量空间
克拉克斯代尔[1]雷声滚滚，一切都那么愁苦
我真的无法快乐，亲爱的
除非你跟我一起快乐
现实真是糟糕
洪水铺天盖地

---

1. 克拉克斯代尔，美国密西西比州城市，三角洲蓝调的发祥地。

High Water
(For Charley Patton)

High water risin'—risin' night and day
All the gold and silver are being stolen away
Big Joe Turner lookin' east and west
From the dark room of his mind
He made it to Kansas City
Twelfth Street and Vine
Nothing standing there
High water everywhere

High water risin', the shacks are slidin' down
Folks lose their possessions—folks are leaving town
Bertha Mason shook it—broke it
Then she hung it on a wall
Says, "You're dancin' with whom they tell you to
Or you don't dance at all."
It's tough out there
High water everywhere

I got a cravin' love for blazing speed
Got a hopped up Mustang Ford
Jump into the wagon, love, throw your panties overboard
I can write you poems, make a strong man lose his mind
I'm no pig without a wig
I hope you treat me kind
Things are breakin' up out there
High water everywhere

High water risin', six inches 'bove my head
Coffins droppin' in the street
Like balloons made out of lead
Water pourin' into Vicksburg, don't know what I'm going
to do
"Don't reach out for me," she said
"Can't you see I'm drownin' too?"
It's rough out there
High water everywhere

Well, George Lewis told the Englishman, the Italian and the
Jew
"Don't open up your mind, boys,
To every conceivable point of view."
They got Charles Darwin trapped out there on Highway
Five
Judge says to the High Sheriff
"I want him dead or alive
Either one, I don't care."
High water everywhere

The Cuckoo is a pretty bird, she warbles as she flies
I'm preachin' the word of God
I'm puttin' out your eyes
I asked Fat Nancy for something to eat, she said, "Take it
off the shelf—
As great as you are, man,
You'll never be greater than yourself."
I told her I didn't really care
High water everywhere

I'm gettin' up in the morning—I believe I'll dust my broom
Keeping away from the women

I'm givin' 'em lots of room
Thunder rolling over Clarksdale, everything is looking blue
I just can't be happy, love
Unless you're happy too
It's bad out there
High water everywhere

月光

四季不停地轮转
我的心一直在渴盼
多想再听到金莺儿那美妙动听的旋律
快来月光下独自和我相遇

光线昏暗，白昼已消散
兰花，虞美人，黑眼睛苏珊菊
大地和天空已骨肉相连融为一体
快来月光下独自和我相遇

夜色浓重又饱满
沿着河堤弥漫
那里的大雁都已经朝着乡间飞去
快来月光下独自和我相遇

啊，我在鼓吹一派祥和
这安宁静谧的恩泽
像一个梦轻轻飘过地板
亲爱的我会带你渡过大河
你没有必要在这里耽搁

放下窗帘吧，快走出门来

云朵渐渐变成枣红
落叶从树干掉到空中
枝条把它们的身影投在了石壁
快来月光下独自和我相遇

柏木成荫的大道
化装舞会上的蜜蜂和小鸟
粉粉白白的花瓣已在风中吹起
快来月光下独自和我相遇

那滋长的青苔和神秘的辉光
紫色花朵轻柔柔的像雪花一样
快动身，把钢镚儿拍进投币口
落日的余晖荧荧不熄
狭窄的路上人潮拥挤
但又有谁在乎你对我究竟原谅与否

我的脉搏在掌心里跳动
陡峭的山峰一座座高耸
金黄的原野上歪扭的老橡树呻吟低语
快来月光下独自和我相遇

Moonlight

The seasons they are turnin'
And my sad heart is yearnin'
To hear again the songbird's sweet melodious tone
Meet me in the moonlight alone

The dusky light, the day is losing
Orchids, poppies, black-eyed Susan
The earth and sky that melts with flesh and bone
Meet me in the moonlight alone

The air is thick and heavy
All along the levee
Where the geese into the countryside have flown
Meet me in the moonlight alone

Well, I'm preachin' peace and harmony
The blessings of tranquility
Floating like a dream across the floor
I'll take you 'cross the river dear
You've no need to linger here
Draw the blinds, step outside the door

The clouds are turnin' crimson
The leaves fall from the limbs an'
The branches cast their shadows over stone
Meet me in the moonlight alone

The boulevards of Cypress trees
The masquerades of birds and bees

The petals, pink and white, the wind has blown
Meet me in the moonlight alone

The trailing moss and mystic glow
Purple blossoms soft as snow
Step up and drop the coin right into the slot
The fading light of sunset glowed
It's crowded on the narrow road
Who cares whether you forgive me or not

My pulse is runnin' through my palm
The sharp hills are rising from
The yellow fields with twisted oaks that groan
Meet me in the moonlight alone

对我一片真心

啊，我的船在这座不夜城搁浅

这里有一些女人只会让我毛骨悚然

我总要想尽办法避开南区

我这样的回忆，真令人窒息

啊，我在夜色最深的时候上岸

尽管你已经努力做好，很多事情还是磕磕绊绊

你无法理解——我对你的感情

要是你明白你就会对我一片真心

我毫不悔恨我做过的任何事情

我真高兴我曾经狠拼——我但求我们能赢

暹罗连体人[1]进城了

市民们迫不及待——他们从四面八方涌来

我离家出走的时候天空裂成了两半

我再也不想回到那里——宁可一刀两段

你无法理解——我对你的感情

要是你明白你就会对我一片真心

---

1. "暹罗连体人"恩昌兄弟（Siamese Twins, Eng & Chang Bunker, 1811—1874），美国著名的连体人表演者。

我的女人那一脸就像泰迪熊

她挥着棒球棍呼呼在空中

一身皮糙肉厚，你用剑都戳不透

我的飞车冲冲撞撞，仪表板插进后备箱

你说我的眼睛迷人我的笑容甜美

啊，我就卖给你吧价廉物美

你无法理解——我对你的感情

要是你明白你就会对我一片真心

有些事情真可怕得难以置信

我不会再来这里如果总是惹你烦心

南太平洋 [1] 九点四十五分开车

我简直无法相信竟然还有人活着

我一丝不挂，但我根本不在乎

我要去森林里，我打猎总是光着屁股 [2]

你无法理解——我对你的感情

啊，要是你明白你就会对我一片真心

我在这里开创新的皇权帝国

---

1. 美国南太平洋铁路公司有列车从中西部（如新奥尔良、堪萨斯）开往加利
福尼亚州。
2. 光着屁股（bare）谐音"熊"（bear），亦即上一段的泰迪熊、我的女人、
性爱。

看情况需要我做的事情还有很多

我对你真的很在乎——从没想过我能做到

我不能对自己的内心说你不好

啊，我的爸妈告诫我不要虚度了年华

但我还是把他们的教导当成耳边的废话

你无法理解——我对你的感情

啊，要是你明白你就会对我一片真心

Honest with Me

Well, I'm stranded in the city that never sleeps
Some of these women they just give me the creeps
I'm avoidin' the Southside the best I can
These memories I got, they can strangle a man
Well, I came ashore in the dead of the night
Lot of things can get in the way when you're tryin' to do
    what's right
You don't understand it—my feelings for you
You'd be honest with me if only you knew

I'm not sorry for nothin' I've done
I'm glad I fought—I only wish we'd won
The Siamese twins are comin' to town
People can't wait—they're gathered around
When I left my home the sky split open wide
I never wanted to go back there—I'd rather have died
You don't understand it—my feelings for you
You'd be honest with me if only you knew

My woman got a face like a teddy bear
She's tossin' a baseball bat in the air
The meat is so tough you can't cut it with a sword
I'm crashin' my car, trunk first into the boards
You say my eyes are pretty and my smile is nice
Well, I'll sell it to ya at a reduced price
You don't understand it—my feelings for you
You'd be honest with me if only you knew

Some things are too terrible to be true

I won't come here no more if it bothers you
The Southern Pacific leaving at nine forty-five
I'm having a hard time believin' some people were ever alive
I'm stark naked, but I don't care
I'm going off into the woods, I'm huntin' bare
You don't understand it—my feelings for you
Well, you'd be honest with me if only you knew

I'm here to create the new imperial empire
I'm going to do whatever circumstances require
I care so much for you—didn't think that I could
I can't tell my heart that you're no good
Well, my parents they warned me not to waste my years
And I still got their advice oozing out of my ears
You don't understand it—my feelings for you
Well, you'd be honest with me if only you knew

苦孩子

有人来敲门——我说："你这是找谁呢？"
他说："你老婆。"我说："她在厨房忙着呢。"
苦孩子，你到哪里去了？
我早跟你说过——不想再多说

我走进商店，说："你要多少钱才肯卖？"
那人说："三块钱。""好吧，"我说，"四块干不干？"
苦孩子，从来不言败
一切都会变好在将来的未来

在大铁路上干活——累得像是玩儿命
游戏总是同样——只有不同的水平
苦孩子，穿一身黑衣
警察就在背后等你

苦孩子在一座红火的城
远过那些闪烁的星
乘上头等列车——周游世界
抓住啊，别掉在车厢之间

奥赛罗对苔丝德蒙娜[1]说："我冷，给我盖床毯子。

还有，那杯毒酒怎样了？"她说："我给过你了，

　　你喝过了。"

苦孩子，把它们摆整齐

盘子上掉的樱桃一颗颗捡起

时间和爱情用它的利爪给我打上烙印

只能跑到佛罗里达，躲开它们佐治亚律法

苦孩子，坐在阴郁中

拨叫客房服务，说："给我送个房间上来。"

我妈妈是一个富农的女儿

我爸爸是旅行推销员，我从没见过他一面

我妈妈死后，舅舅收养了我——他是开殡仪馆的

他为我做了很多好事，我不会忘记他

我只记得你的吻心荡神驰

除此之外我一无所知

苦孩子，捡起树棍吧

给你盖一幢房子用灰泥和砖瓦

---

1. 在莎士比亚悲剧《奥赛罗》中，奥赛罗因受奸人蛊惑而掐死了爱妻苔丝德
蒙娜，奥赛罗知道真相后也自刎而死。歌中的对话与莎剧无关。

听见敲门声，我说："你是谁、你从哪里来？"

那人说："弗雷迪！"我说："哪个弗雷迪呀？"他说：

"弗雷迪了吗，我来了。"[1]

苦孩子，夜空里星光簇簇

给他们洗碗，给他们喂猪

---

1. 以上两行歌词源自英文笑话，"弗雷迪"（Freddy）谐音"准备"（ready）。

Po' Boy

Man comes to the door—I say, "For whom are you
  looking?"
He says, "Your wife." I say, "She's busy in the kitchen
  cookin'."
Poor boy, where you been?
I already tol' you—won't tell you again

I say, "How much you want for that?" I go into the store
The man says, "Three dollars." "All right," I say, "Will you
  take four?"
Poor boy, never say die
Things will be all right by and by

Been workin' on the mainline—workin' like the devil
The game is the same—it's just up on a different level
Poor boy, dressed in black
Police at your back

Poor boy in a red hot town
Out beyond the twinklin' stars
Ridin' first class trains—making the rounds
Tryin' to keep from fallin' between the cars

Othello told Desdemona, "I'm cold, cover me with
  a blanket.
By the way, what happened to that poison wine?" She says, "I
  gave it to you, you drank it."
Poor boy, layin' 'em straight
Pickin' up the cherries fallin' off the plate

Time and love has branded me with its claws
Had to go to Florida, dodgin' them Georgia laws
Poor boy, sitting in the gloom
Calls down to room service, says, "Send up a room."

My mother was a daughter of a wealthy farmer
My father was a traveling salesman, I never met him
When my mother died, my uncle took me in—he ran a
    funeral parlor
He did a lot of nice things for me and I won't forget him

All I know is that I'm thrilled by your kiss
I don't know any more than this
Poor boy, pickin' up sticks
Build ya a house out of mortar and bricks

Knockin' on the door, I say, "Who is it and where are you
    from?"
Man says, "Freddy!" I say, "Freddy who?" He says, "Freddy
    or not here I come."
Poor boy, 'neath the stars that shine
Washin' them dishes, feedin' them swine

哭一会吧

啊，我必须出趟门，去见一个家伙名叫戈德史密斯
　　先生[1]
一个背信弃义、下流无耻、两面三刀的卑鄙小人我才
　　懒得跟他折腾
但我为你做了而你给我的回报只有一个微笑
啊，我为你哭过——现在轮到你哭一会吧

我已经不堪负累——我不是昙花一现
好吧，我给你说清楚，你没看出来吗我是工会成员？
我把猫咪放出笼子[2]，我总保持低调
啊，我为你哭过——现在轮到你了，哭一会吧

感觉像一只好斗的公鸡——感觉从来没这么爽过
但宾夕法尼亚干线乱七八糟，丹佛铁路一塌糊涂
我到教堂去了，每一天我多走一里路
啊，我为你哭过——现在轮到你了，哭一会吧

----

1. 哈维·戈德史密斯（Harvey Goldsmith, 1946— ），英国著名摇滚演唱
会策划人。
2. 把猫咪放出笼子，改自习语"让猫咪从口袋里出来"（let the cat out of
the bag），意为无意中泄露机密、揭露真相。

昨晚在后巷那边传来轰轰的砸墙声

肯定是帕斯夸列老爷[1]凌晨两点约上了一炮

你的风格就是碾碎一颗像我这样天真的心

啊，我为你哭过——现在轮到你哭一会吧

我在夜的边缘，抵抗我无法控制的眼泪

有些人根本不是人类，他们没有心或者灵魂

啊，我向上帝哭诉——我尽量温和又温顺

真的，我为你哭过——现在轮到你了，哭一会吧

啊，牧师都在讲台上，宝宝都在马槽里

我只想要你的肋骨下面的那块嫩嫩肉

我要给自己买一桶威士忌——在衰老之前我会死去

啊，我为你哭过——现在轮到你了，哭一会吧

啊，你下注的赛马总是跑错方向

我一直说你会后悔的，今天就是时候了

我可能需要一个好律师，也许就在你的葬礼、我的审判

啊，我为你哭过，现在轮到你了，哭一会吧

---

1. 帕斯夸列老爷，出自意大利歌剧作曲家葛塔诺·多尼采蒂（Gaetano Donizetti）同名歌剧中的一个单身老地主。

Cry a While

Well, I had to go down and see a guy named Mr. Goldsmith
A nasty, dirty, double-crossin', back-stabbin' phony I didn't
    wanna have to be dealin' with
But I did it for you and all you gave me was a smile
Well, I cried for you—now it's your turn to cry awhile

I don't carry dead weight—I'm no flash in the pan
All right, I'll set you straight, can't you see I'm a union
    man?
I'm lettin' the cat out of the cage, I'm keeping a low profile
Well, I cried for you—now it's your turn, you can cry
    awhile

Feel like a fighting rooster—feel better than I ever felt
But the Pennsylvania line's in an awful mess and the Denver
    road is about to melt
I went to the church house, every day I go an extra mile
Well, I cried for you—now it's your turn, you can cry
    awhile

Last night 'cross the alley there was a pounding on the walls
It must have been Don Pasqualli makin' a two A.M. booty
    call
To break a trusting heart like mine was just your style
Well, I cried for you—now it's your turn to cry awhile

I'm on the fringes of the night, fighting back tears that I
    can't control
Some people they ain't human, they got no heart or soul

Well, I'm crying to the Lord—I'm tryin' to be meek and
   mild
Yes, I cried for you—now it's your turn, you can cry awhile

Well, there's preachers in the pulpits and babies in the cribs
I'm longin' for that sweet fat that sticks to your ribs
I'm gonna buy me a barrel of whiskey—I'll die before I turn
   senile
Well, I cried for you—now it's your turn, you can cry
   awhile

Well, you bet on a horse and it ran on the wrong way
I always said you'd be sorry and today could be the day
I might need a good lawyer, could be your funeral, my trial
Well, I cried for you—now it's your turn, you can cry
   awhile

甜妞宝贝

我转身背对着太阳因为阳光实在太刺眼
我能看见世界上每一个人都在面临着什么
你不能后退——你不能重回，有时我们已走得太远
有一天你会睁开眼你就会看见我们处在什么地方

甜妞宝贝一路向前
你不要没头没脑
你已经离开我多年
不妨就这样继续向前

这些走私贩子，他们有时真能搞出上好的货色
很多地方可以藏东西只要你真的敢做敢想
我跟莎莉姨妈在一块，但你知道，她其实不是我姨妈
这些回忆有的你能学着去接受有的却不行

甜妞宝贝一直向前
你不要没头没脑
你已经离开我多年
不妨就这样继续向前

黑人区的女士，她们在跳黑人区阔步

你始终做好准备但你不知道是为了什么

女人带来的烦恼，其总量真是没有上限

爱是取悦，爱是挑逗，爱不是邪恶的事情

甜妞宝贝，一路向前

你不要没头没脑

你已经离开我多年

不妨就这样继续向前

存在的每一个瞬间都仿佛卑鄙的花招

幸福会突然降临又猛然间离去

无论在怎样的时刻气泡都有可能破碎

尽量为某人做点好事吧，尽管到头来你经常会让事情

　　坏上一千倍

甜妞宝贝，一路向前

你不要没头没脑

你已经离开我多年

不妨就这样继续向前

你的魅力已经粉碎了许多颗心，我当然就是其一

你掌握了一种把世界撕裂的方法，亲爱的，瞧你干了些
　　什么
就像我们活着一样的真，就像你诞生一样的真
看天上，看天上——寻找你的造物主——在加百列吹响
　　号角之前

甜妞宝贝，一直向前
你不要没头没脑
你已经离开我多年
不妨就这样继续向前

Sugar Baby

I got my back to the sun 'cause the light is too intense
I can see what everybody in the world is up against
You can't turn back—you can't come back, sometimes we
  push too far
One day you'll open up your eyes and you'll see where
  we are

Sugar Baby get on down the road
You ain't got no brains, no how
You went years without me
Might as well keep going now

Some of these bootleggers, they make pretty good stuff
Plenty of places to hide things here if you wanna hide 'em
  bad enough
I'm staying with Aunt Sally, but you know, she's not really
  my aunt
Some of these memories you can learn to live with and some
  of them you can't

Sugar Baby get on down the line
You ain't got no brains, no how
You went years without me
You might as well keep going now

The ladies in Darktown, they're doing the Darktown Strut
You always got to be prepared but you never know for what
There ain't no limit to the amount of trouble women bring
Love is pleasing, love is teasing, love's not an evil thing

Sugar Baby, get on down the road
You ain't got no brains, no how
You went years without me
You might as well keep going now

Every moment of existence seems like some dirty trick
Happiness can come suddenly and leave just as quick
Any minute of the day the bubble could burst
Try to make things better for someone, sometimes you just
    end up making it a thousand times worse

Sugar Baby, get on down the road
You ain't got no brains, no how
You went years without me
Might as well keep going now

Your charms have broken many a heart and mine is surely
    one
You got a way of tearing a world apart, love, see what you
    done
Just as sure as we're living, just as sure as you're born
Look up, look up—seek your Maker—'fore Gabriel blows
    his horn

Sugar Baby, get on down the line
You ain't got no sense, no how
You went years without me
Might as well keep going now

走过青山绿岭 [1]

（电影《众神与将军》插曲）

我走过青山绿岭，我露宿溪流之滨

天堂在头脑里燃烧，我从一场噩梦中惊醒

从海底闯出的鬼怪东西

肆虐在富裕和自由的土地

我看着我的朋友安详地闭上眼睛

然后我问自己，是否已到绝境？

回忆挥之不去，悲伤又甜蜜

我想到灵魂上了天堂还会相遇

祭坛在烈火中分崩离析

从河对面已经扑来了仇敌

在山顶上他们脱帽致意

热血又将抛洒，你感到了杀气

---

1. 这首歌所述内容与影片情节有关。《众神与将军》（*Gods and Generals*，
2003）一片描述了美国南北战争初期双方忠勇将士们的群像，较倾向南军的
意识形态，尤其关注了南军名将"石墙"杰克逊（Stonewall Jackson）的
传奇生涯。

沿着昏暗的大西洋铁路

被蹂躏的土地远远地起伏

大道笔直宽畅，前方总有光明

一切都必须服从上帝的报应

世界太沧桑，世界太灰暗

人生的功课不可能一天就学完

我坚守着我瞭望我谛听我在等待

有音乐从那遥远的幸福之乡传来

让我们的队长合眼吧，但愿他安息

他的长夜结束了，伟大领袖已经倒地

他对失败从不畏惧，他会立刻组织反击

当场杀死他的却是他自己的士兵 [1]

最后的快乐岁月的最后一天最后一刻

我感到那未知的世界近在眼前

骄傲会磨灭，荣耀会腐朽

但美德不会被遗忘，它万古永久

晚祷的钟声已经敲响

---

1. "石墙"杰克逊以防守反击而成名，最后在一次夜巡中被己方误击重伤而死。

每一张嘴都在亵渎神灵

任他们去说我走在美如仙境的光明

说我忠于真理忠于正义

侍奉上帝并满心喜乐，抬头仰望远方

远过那遮蔽了黎明破晓的沉沉黑暗

在鲜血浸泡的树林有深绿色的草木

他们从没想过屈服。他们倒在他们站立之处

群星陨落亚拉巴马，每颗星我都看清

无论是谁你都是在睡梦中旅行

寒冷的是诸天，刺骨的是霜雪

大地冻得僵硬而早晨迟迟不再出现

写给妈妈的信今天才送到

胸口中了一枪，信中说道

但他很快会好的他已经躺在病房

但他永远不会好了，他已经死亡

我远在城市几十里外，我已飞走

在一种远古的光明中没有了白昼

他们冷静，他们迟钝，我们实在太了解

我们互相深爱对方，比我们敢说的更深切

'Cross the Green Mountain
(from the film *Gods and Generals*)

I crossed the green mountain, I slept by the stream
Heaven blazin' in my head, I dreamt a monstrous dream
Something came up out of the sea
Swept through the land of the rich and the free

I look into the eyes of my merciful friend
And then I ask myself, is this the end?
Memories linger, sad yet sweet
And I think of the souls in heaven who will meet

Altars are burning with flames falling wide
The foe has crossed over from the other side
They tip their caps from the top of the hill
You can feel them come, more brave blood to spill

Along the dim Atlantic line
The ravaged land lies for miles behind
The light's comin' forward and the streets are broad
All must yield to the avenging God

The world is old, the world is gray
Lessons of life can't be learned in a day
I watch and I wait and I listen while I stand
To the music that comes from a far better land

Close the eyes of our Captain, peace may he know
His long night is done, the great leader is laid low

He was ready to fall, he was quick to defend
Killed outright he was by his own men

It's the last day's last hour of the last happy year
I feel that the unknown world is so near
Pride will vanish and glory will rot
But virtue lives and cannot be forgot

The bells of evening have rung
There's blasphemy on every tongue
Let them say that I walked in fair nature's light
And that I was loyal to truth and to right

Serve God and be cheerful, look upward beyond
Beyond the darkness that masks the surprises of dawn
In the deep green grasses of the blood stained wood
They never dreamed of surrendering. They fell where they
    stood

Stars fell over Alabama, I saw each star
You're walkin' in dreams whoever you are
Chilled are the skies, keen is the frost
The ground's froze hard and the morning is lost

A letter to mother came today
Gunshot wound to the breast is what it did say
But he'll be better soon he's in a hospital bed
But he'll never be better, he's already dead

I'm ten miles outside the city and I'm lifted away
In an ancient light that is not of day
They were calm, they were blunt, we knew 'em all too well
We loved each other more than we ever dared to tell

等着你

（电影《丫丫姐妹们的神圣秘密》插曲）

我从没梦想过有个人是为我专门定做

我不会让她如愿以偿

我来这儿看看她有什么要讲

哦，可怜的小妞总能赢得全场

我保持领先，她也旗鼓相当

然后威士忌飞进了我的脑袋

提琴师的胳膊已经瘫痪

而谈话越来越放开

我们的爱情何时已经变坏？

我从前最好的朋友遭遇了什么事变？

已经很久了我不再紧紧拥抱你

已经很久了我们不再说晚安

眼泪的滋味又苦又甜

当你靠近我，我的心忘记怎样跳动

每个夜晚你都处在善和真当中

我会在身边，等着你

他们的大王已经开始倒台

在船夫舞会上我失去了我的姑娘

夜晚有一千颗心一千只眼睛

希望会消逝但绝不会死

明天我还会见你当自由之声响起

我要去站在事物之巅

当仲夏之夜，蓝月亮高挂天际

我会在身边等着你

又一局输掉，又一个人走掉

你忍受着一切，你继续向前

有些事情阻拦你但你会克服过去

我把全世界以及一切都押在你身上

幸福不过是一种心理状态

你随时都可以跨过边界

你不需要多么富有或者发大财

我会在身边等着你

Waitin' for You

(from the film *Divine Secrets of the Ya-Ya Sisterhood*)

I never dreamed there could be someone made just for me
I'm not letting her have her way
I come here to see what she has to say
Oh, the poor gal always wins the day
I'm staying ahead of the game, she's doing the same
And the whiskey's flying into my head
The fiddler's arm has gone dead
And talk is beginning to spread

When did our love go bad?
Whatever happened to the best friend that I had?
Been so long since I held you tight
Been so long since we said goodnight
The taste of tears is bittersweet
When you're near me, my heart forgets to beat
You're there every night among the good and the true
And I'll be around, waitin' for you

The king of them all is starting to fall
I lost my gal at the boatman's ball
The night has a thousand hearts and eyes
Hope may vanish but it never dies
I'll see you tomorrow when freedom rings
I'm gonna stay on top of things
It's the middle of the summer and the moon is blue
I'll be around waitin' for you

Another deal gone down, another man done gone
You put up with it all and you carry on
Something holding you back but you'll come through
I'd bet the world and everything in it on you
Happiness is but a state of mind
Anytime you want you can cross the state line
You don't need to be rich or well-to-do
I'll be around waitin' for you

1. Lost John, sitting on the railroad track / Something's out of whack
Blues this morning falling down like hail
Gonna leave a greasy trail

2. Gonna travel the world is what I'm going to do / then come back and see you
Days creep by, each one feels like a year   (many more years)
So many things come to nothing I could here

3. I'm the oldest son of a crazy man / I'm in a cowboy band
Got a pile of sins to pay for and I ain't got time to hide
I'd walk thru a blazing fire baby if I knew you was on the other side

4. Going when the Southern crosses the Yellow Dog / to get away from those demagogues   on
Ain't these bad luck women that stick (to you) like glue   let's go down   Stopping all my thoughts before
Always getting in the way when there's work to do   they start to run ...
                                                                                                                                    looking at em all's annoying
                                                                                                    (let's go down to Jacksonville) went parking hell   (   )
5. Dr. Frankenstein's   styling   up there at his castle on the hill / up there still (with all moons(kiss shell) she's dy
At best in the graveyard, Frankie's raising hell   (I'm going to Jackson ville) (cathouse woman 'n' hod-
I'm beginning to believe (empty tree) what the scriptures fell   they saving all day
                                                                                                                                                                    (on

6. She says "look out Daddy, don't want ya to tear your pants! / you could get wrecked in this dance "
They say that whiskey'll kill ya but i don't think it will
You went away 'n' left me but i believe you love me still

7. It's getting light outside, the temperature dropped / i think the rain has stopped   It's   (been
I'm going to wake you come to grips with fate   It can (run the worm
When I'm thru with you, you'll learn how to keep your business straight   begin
                                                                                                                        f a c

8. the judge is comin', all rise / lift up your eyes
I went to the river, threw away my dice
Before you call me any dirty names, you better think twice

9. Don't know why my baby went cooked so good baby / i don't have to wonder no more
She been cookin' all day and it's gonna take me all night   your sweet lovin'   his elegant (nf. girl)
I can't eat it all but (it) don't it's gonna take me in a single bite   sorry -

10. Today I'm stand in faith and raise / the voice of praise   (you're inside all day   sorry) Every kind of grief gives way -
My head would go astray (they say) (you want when go astray)   i could hang up away
A lifetime with you is like some heavenly day   Donated to my orphan army   A cathouse
                                                                                                                                            woman 'n' A
11. Everything I've ever known to be right has been proven wrong / I'll be driftin' along   god gifted man
I went to tuedance / wore out my shoes   go head in head --
She says " dont worry (bout it) Daddy, i dont you know you can't lose "   shooting my spots in the
                                                                                                                                sky
12. The bright spark of the steady lights / has veiled the day's distracting sights   (no one within in sight)
I know you'd never thrown me down (I'll be lovin' you when my wheelbarrow touch the ground)
when you die, I'll keep hanging around --   (that   I'm that many lives - c'mon   (never throwed
*   dim)   i was born on high ground   you down-
                                                                                                     I'm stuck with you -babe

13. Lost John — 1st verse —

摩登时代

Modern Times

陈震 译

　　2006 年 8 月底，六十五岁的鲍勃·迪伦发表了五年来的首张录音室专辑《摩登时代》。老而弥坚的迪伦，总是不断带给我们各种惊奇。之前的五年里，除了密集巡演，他还写了一本自传，参与了马丁·斯科塞斯执导的关于他的传记电影《没有回家的路》(No Direction Home)。而《摩登时代》亦以转变之姿，取得了商业和口碑的巨大成功，一举登上多国专辑榜的冠军宝座，也让迪伦以六十五岁高龄，成为最年长的《公告牌》专辑榜冠军得主。

　　《摩登时代》由迪伦亲自担纲制作，里面既有躁动热烈的电声蓝调，又有舒缓温柔的抒情歌谣。不同以往的是，专辑中几乎每一首歌，都有旋律借鉴自前人的经典名曲。这令此张专辑也颇具争议。但录音乐手们的演奏功力和那些乐句的历史底蕴实在深厚，令听者不由得陶醉其中，跟着律动摇晃起来，浑然忘了去辨别一首首歌分别改编自哪首名曲。《摩登时代》采用的是模拟录音，由一支"世界上最伟大的酒吧乐队"实时合奏录制而成，这让这张录音室专辑听起来犹如现场般肆意直接。

生与死、爱与恨依然在他的歌声中缠绕。从对爱人的渴望，到想要报复的仇恨，再到对死亡的思索，迪伦满脑子的奇思妙想在他机智的戏谑、预言式的比喻中得以舒张。而除了情爱纠缠和宗教意象，还有与这个时代切肤相关的主题，以及对这个世界糟糕现况的影射。

陈震

山上的雷声

山上的雷声，月上的火焰

巷里在骚动，太阳将出现

今天这日子，要抓起长号吹

哦，这儿有辣妹，她们无处不在

我在想艾丽西亚·凯斯[1]，忍不住哭了出来

她降生在地狱厨房[2]时，我就住在那一带

我想知道艾丽西亚·凯斯究竟在哪里

为了找她我甚至翻遍了田纳西

感觉我的灵魂开始扩大

窥视我的心，你会有点明白

是你把我带到这里，现在你又让我离开

厄运之兆[3]已经显露，来读下，看看写的啥

---

1. 艾丽西亚·凯斯（Alicia Keys，1981— ），美国创作型女歌手、演员。
2. 地狱厨房，纽约市曼哈顿西岸的一个地区，早年是贫穷的爱尔兰裔劳工阶层的聚集地，曾被认为是曼哈顿治安最差、黑帮云集的一区。但该地段邻近百老汇剧院和演员工作室，亦吸引不少演艺学生、新人居住。歌手艾丽西亚·凯斯便是在地狱厨房出生、成长，迪伦也曾在这一地区居住。
3. 厄运之兆，直译为"写在墙上的文字"，《旧约·但以理书》5:5-28，伯沙撒王的宴会上，"忽有人的指头显出，在王宫与灯台相对的墙上写字"，但以理为王解读文字，说神预告了其国的终结。

山上的雷声，滚滚如擂鼓

要睡在那里，音乐从那来

我不需要向导，我已经认识路

记住我是你的家仆，朝朝暮暮

枪声大作，灯火齐暗

我想尝试些什么，但我离市区好远

阳光依旧闪耀，北风依旧呼啸

我会暂时忘掉自己，去看别人需要什么

我坐着研习爱的艺术

我想这非常适合我

想找个好女人照着我的话去做

谁都会困惑这个残酷的世界怎么了

山上的雷声，滚落到地上

将一早起床，踏上坎坷路

在美好的一天，我会站在我的国王旁边

我不会背叛你的爱，或其他任何东西

将招募一大队人马，一帮狠劲十足的狗娘养的

将从孤儿院征召我的部队

我去过圣赫尔曼教堂，立过宗教誓言

我吸了一千头母牛的奶

我有猪排，她有派

她不是天使，我也不是

你的贪婪真可耻，你的诡计真丢脸
我才不在乎你的梦想呢

山上的雷声，沉重地滚动
凶恶的老旋风，一步步逼近
华盛顿的所有女士争先恐后地出城
看起来像有坏事发生，飞机最好变向
人人都在跑，我也想跟上
不想和陌生人冒这个险
我尽我所能，立刻去做
我已经忏悔过，没必要再忏悔
要赚大钱，要去北方
种地，收获地里长出来的东西
锤子在桌上，干草叉在架上
看在上帝的份上，你应该怜悯你自己

Thunder on the Mountain

Thunder on the mountain, fires on the moon
There's a ruckus in the alley and the sun will be here soon
Today's the day, gonna grab my trombone and blow
Well, there's hot stuff here and it's everywhere I go
I was thinkin' 'bout Alicia Keys, couldn't keep from crying
When she was born in Hell's Kitchen, I was living down the
    line
I'm wondering where in the world Alicia Keys could be
I been looking for her even clear through Tennessee
Feel like my soul is beginning to expand
Look into my heart and you will sort of understand
You brought me here, now you're trying to run me away
The writing's on the wall, come read it, come see what it say

Thunder on the mountain, rolling like a drum
Gonna sleep over there, that's where the music coming from
I don't need any guide, I already know the way
Remember this, I'm your servant both night and day
The pistols are poppin' and the power is down
I'd like to try somethin' but I'm so far from town
The sun keeps shinin' and the North Wind keeps picking
    up speed
Gonna forget about myself for a while, gonna go out and
    see what others need
I've been sitting down studying the art of love
I think it will fit me like a glove
I want some real good woman to do just what I say
Everybody got to wonder what's the matter with this cruel
    world today

Thunder on the mountain rolling to the ground
Gonna get up in the morning walk the hard road down
Some sweet day I'll stand beside my king
I wouldn't betray your love or any other thing
Gonna raise me an army, some tough sons of bitches
I'll recruit my army from the orphanages
I been to St. Herman's church and I've said my religious
  vows
I've sucked the milk out of a thousand cows
I got the porkchops, she got the pie
She ain't no angel and neither am I
Shame on your greed, shame on your wicked schemes
I'll say this, I don't give a damn about your dreams

Thunder on the mountain heavy as can be
Mean old twister bearing down on me
All the ladies of Washington scrambling to get out of town
Looks like something bad gonna happen, better roll your
  airplane down
Everybody's going and I want to go too
Don't wanna take a chance with somebody new
I did all I could and I did it right there and then
I've already confessed—no need to confess again
Gonna make a lot of money, gonna go up north
I'll plant and I'll harvest what the earth brings forth
The hammer's on the table, the pitchfork's on the shelf
For the love of God, you ought to take pity on yourself

灵在水上

灵在水上

黑暗在渊面 [1]

我一直在想你，宝贝

几乎无法入睡

我游走在大地

走过晨曦

你常在我心里

挥不去离不开

我忘掉过你

你又不期而来

我早就明白

我们注定不只是朋友而已

当你近在咫尺

这完全一目了然

我为你着迷，女孩

你也应该为我犯傻

无法解释

1.《旧约·创世记》1:2 ："地是空虚混沌，渊面黑暗；上帝的灵运行在水面上。"

这种隐秘痛楚的根源

你烧出一条进入我心的路

你有了开启我大脑的钥匙

我脚踏烂泥

祈求上苍

我万分紧张

你脸上写着爱的乞望

生命中没有你

一切皆无意义

如果不能拥有你

我就把爱扔进深蓝海底

有时我在想

你为何不能好好待我

你白天做得很好

晚上又做得很差

当我和你在一起

我的快乐无法用言语表达

那又有什么关系

我付出了什么代价

他们吹嘘你甜得像糖

满街满城地吹嘘

往我碗里放些糖

我想跟你上床

我苍白如鬼

握着一根茎上的一簇花朵

你见过鬼吗？没

但你听说过

你的名字

在我耳边萦绕

我说得很明了

这些纽带足够牢靠

卷入了一场争吵

现在我已无力向前

我要离开了，宝贝

秋天才回来

山岗之上

请带走我对你的惦念

你麻木了我的意志

这份爱能把我撕成两片

我想和你同在天堂

这似乎太不公平

我再也回不了天堂

我在那儿杀了一个人

你以为我盛年不再

你以为我宝刀已老

让我瞧瞧你厉不厉害

我们能玩得无比痛快

Spirit on the Water

Spirit on the water
Darkness on the face of the deep
I keep thinking about you baby
I can't hardly sleep
I'm traveling by land
Traveling through the dawn of day
You're always on my mind
I can't stay away
I'd forgotten about you
Then you turned up again
I always knew
That we were meant to be more than friends
When you are near
It's just as plain as it can be
I'm wild about you, gal
You ought to be a fool about me

Can't explain
The sources of this hidden pain
You burned your way into my heart
You got the key to my brain
I've been trampling through mud
Praying to the powers above
I'm sweating blood
You got a face that begs for love
Life without you
Doesn't mean a thing to me
If I can't have you
I'll throw my love into the deep blue sea

Sometimes I wonder
Why you can't treat me right
You do good all day
Then you do wrong all night

When you're with me
I'm a thousand times happier than I could ever say
What does it matter
What price I pay
They brag about your sugar
Brag about it all over town
Put some sugar in my bowl
I feel like laying down
I'm pale as a ghost
Holding a blossom on a stem
You ever seen a ghost? No
But you have heard of them
I hear your name
Ringing up and down the line
I'm saying it plain
These ties are strong enough to bind

I been in a brawl
Now I'm feeling the wall
I'm going away baby
I won't be back 'til fall
High on the hill
You can carry all my thoughts with you
You've numbed my will
This love could tear me in two
I wanna be with you in paradise
And it seems so unfair
I can't go back to paradise no more

I killed a man back there
You think I'm over the hill
You think I'm past my prime
Let me see what you got
We can have a whoppin' good time

跌跌撞撞，踉踉跄跄

我跌跌撞撞，踉踉跄跄，整夜都在哭
我跌跌撞撞，踉踉跄跄，整夜都在哭
我早上醒来，我一定下错了注

我麻烦缠身，不堪重负
我麻烦缠身，不堪重负
某个又懒又骚的小娘们勾走了我的魂

风景在白天的金光下微微发亮
风景在白天的金光下微微发亮
现在我不碍任何人的事，不挡任何人的路

我彻底没力气了，这娘们把我弄哭了
我彻底没力气了，这娘们她把我弄哭了
这娘们太疯狂了，我发誓这几年不会沾惹别人

哦，暖和天来了，葡萄藤发芽了
暖和天来了，葡萄藤发芽了
没什么比试图满足我这娘们更令人沮丧

我早上醒来，看到旭日回来了

哦，我早上醒来，看到旭日回来了

早晚有一天你也要晒伤

夜晚充满了阴影，岁月充满了提早的劫数

夜晚充满了阴影，岁月充满了提早的劫数

我一直在施法召唤这些老亡灵，从他们摇摇欲坠的坟墓

让我们互相原谅，亲爱的，让我们去绿林峡谷

让我们互相原谅，亲爱的，让我们去绿林峡谷

让我们一起出主意，让我们做个了断

我跌跌撞撞，踉踉跄跄，整夜都在哭

啊，我跌跌撞撞，踉踉跄跄，整夜都在哭

我早上醒来，我一定跑错了地方

Rollin' and Tumblin'

I rolled and I tumbled, I cried the whole night long
I rolled and I tumbled, I cried the whole night long
Woke up this mornin', I must have bet my money wrong

I got troubles so hard, I can't stand the strain
I got troubles so hard, I just can't stand the strain
Some young lazy slut has charmed away my brains

The landscape is glowin', gleamin' in the golden light of day
The landscape is glowin', gleamin' in the gold light of day
I ain't holding nothin' back now, I ain't standin' in
    anybody's way

I'm flat out spent, this woman been drivin' me to tears
I'm flat out spent, this woman she been drivin' me to tears
This woman so crazy, I swear I ain't gonna touch another
    one for years

Well, the warm weather is comin' and the buds are on the vine
The warm weather's comin', the buds are on the vine
Ain't nothing so depressing as trying to satisfy this woman
    of mine

I got up this mornin', saw the rising sun return
Well, I got up this mornin', seen the rising sun return
Sooner or later you too shall burn

The night's filled with shadows, the years are filled with
    early doom

The night's filled with shadows, the years are filled with
    early doom
I've been conjuring up all these long dead souls from their
    crumblin' tombs

Let's forgive each other darlin', let's go down to the
    greenwood glen
Let's forgive each other darlin', let's go down to the
    greenwood glen
Let's put our heads together, let's put old matters to an end

Now I rolled and I tumbled and I cried the whole night
    long
Ah, I rolled and I tumbled, I cried the whole night long
I woke up this morning, I think I must be travelin' wrong

当交易达成

寂静的夜里，古老的光中
智慧在争斗中成长
我劳而无获，一头雾水
穿过生命之径的漆黑
每个看不见的祈祷都像一朵天上的云
明日总是峰回路转
我们生老病死，我们搞不明白
但当交易达成，我会与你同在

我们吃吃喝喝，感受思考
迷失在街的远方
我又哭又笑
被我从没打算说也不想说的事困扰
午夜的雨追随着列车
我们戴着一样的荆冠
灵魂相拥，影子移动
当交易达成，我会与你同在

月亮发光，夜里皓亮
我却几乎感觉不到

我们学习生活，然后学习宽恕

在这段必将走上的路途

比花朵还要脆弱，这些珍贵的时光

将我们紧紧捆绑

你映入我的眼帘，像天空中的幻象

当交易达成，我会与你同在

我拾起一朵玫瑰，它刺破了我的衣裳

我沿着蜿蜒的小溪

听到震耳的响声，感到片刻的欢畅

我知道它们并非表面模样

在这充满失望和痛楚的凡尘

你永远看不到我眉头皱紧

我亏欠你一颗心，这明明白白

当交易达成，我会与你同在

When the Deal Goes Down

In the still of the night, in the world's ancient light
Where wisdom grows up in strife
My bewildering brain, toils in vain
Through the darkness on the pathways of life
Each invisible prayer is like a cloud in the air
Tomorrow keeps turning around
We live and we die, we know not why
But I'll be with you when the deal goes down

We eat and we drink, we feel and we think
Far down the street we stray
I laugh and I cry and I'm haunted by
Things I never meant nor wished to say
The midnight rain follows the train
We all wear the same thorny crown
Soul to soul, our shadows roll
And I'll be with you when the deal goes down

The moon gives light and shines by night
I scarcely feel the glow
We learn to live and then we forgive
O'er the road we're bound to go
More frailer than the flowers, these precious hours
That keep us so tightly bound
You come to my eyes like a vision from the skies
And I'll be with you when the deal goes down

I picked up a rose and it poked through my clothes
I followed the winding stream

I heard the deafening noise, I felt transient joys
I know they're not what they seem
In this earthly domain, full of disappointment and pain
You'll never see me frown
I owe my heart to you, and that's sayin' it true
And I'll be with you when the deal goes down

宝贝儿，总有一天

我不在乎你做什么，我不在乎你说什么
我不在乎你去哪里，我不在乎你待多久
宝贝儿，总有一天，你不会再为我挂念

哦，你拿走我的钱，逐我出家门
让自我怀疑充斥于我的身体
宝贝儿，总有一天，你不会再为我挂念

当我年轻时，我渴望上路
你逼人太甚，几乎把我逼进坟墓
宝贝儿，总有一天，你不会再为我挂念

有什么地方不对劲，我的心七上八下
我不停地翻新同样的老想法
宝贝儿，总有一天，你不会再为我挂念

我忽略了生命中太多美好的东西
我不知如何是好，我已经为你沉迷
宝贝儿，总有一天，你不会再为我挂念

我要振作起来，我要拧断你的脖子
实在不行的话，我会让它关乎尊严
宝贝儿，总有一天，你不会再为我挂念

带走你的衣衫，装进麻袋
沿着这条路走吧，宝贝儿，不能回来
宝贝儿，总有一天，你不会再为我挂念

我试着变得友善，试着变得友爱
现在我要把你逐出你家，就像当初我被逐出我家
宝贝儿，总有一天，你不会再为我挂念

Someday Baby

I don't care what you do, I don't care what you say
I don't care where you go or how long you stay
Someday baby, you ain't gonna worry po' me anymore

Well you take my money and you turn me out
You fill me up with nothin' but self doubt
Someday baby, you ain't gonna worry po' me anymore

When I was young, driving was my crave
You drive me so hard, almost to the grave
Someday baby, you ain't gonna worry po' me anymore

Something is the matter, my mind tied up in knots
I keep recycling the same old thoughts
Someday baby, you ain't gonna worry po' me anymore

So many good things in life I overlooked
I don't know what to do now, you got me so hooked
Someday baby, you ain't gonna worry po' me anymore

Gonna get myself together, I'm gonna ring your neck
When all else fails I'll make it a matter of self-respect
Someday baby, you ain't gonna worry po' me anymore

You can take your clothes, put 'm in a sack
You goin' down the road, baby and you can't come back
Someday baby, you ain't gonna worry po' me anymore

I try to be friendly, I try to be kind

Now I'm gonna drive you from your home, just like I was
    driven from mine
Someday baby, you ain't gonna worry po' me anymore

劳工蓝调二号

夜晚的薄雾笼罩着小镇

溪边泛着星光

无产阶级的购买力在下降

金钱变得疲软

我最爱的地方已成甜美的回忆

这是一条我们踏上的新路

他们说低薪已成事实

如果我们想同国外竞争

我的凶残武器已被搁置

来，坐我腿上

我爱你胜过爱自己

正如你看到的那样

我听着铁轨嗡嗡作响

两眼紧闭

试图阻止饥饿感

蹑手蹑脚地爬进胃肠

在底下等我，别落在后头

带上我的靴和鞋

在前线时你可以退却或战斗

唱一小段劳工蓝调

我起帆回航，征途漫漫

抛下这里的一切

待在这儿我会失去所有

盗贼将把我抢个精光

我设法往灵魂里添加思想

将睡着度过余下的半天

有时没人稀罕我们的物件

有时你白送都没人要

我早上醒来，一跃而起

心血来潮地去了城里

我在街上看到了父亲

至少我认为是他

黑暗中我听到夜莺啼鸣

群山崎岖陡峭

我睡在厨房，脚伸进门厅

如果我把我的故事全讲给你听，你会哭泣

在底下等我，别落在后头

带上我的靴和鞋

Sometimes nobody wants what you got
Sometimes you can't give it away

I woke up this morning and sprang to my feet
Went into town on a whim
I saw my father there in the street
At least I think it was him
In the dark I hear the night birds call
The hills are rugged and steep
I sleep in the kitchen with my feet in the hall
If I told you my whole story you'd weep

Meet me at the bottom, don't lag behind
Bring me my boots and shoes
You can hang back or fight your best on the front line
Sing a little bit of these workingman's blues

They burned my barn and they stole my horse
I can't save a dime
It's a long way down and I don't want to be forced
Into a life of continual crime
I can see for myself that the sun is sinking
O'er the banks of the deep blue sea
Tell me, am I wrong in thinking
That you have forgotten me

Now they worry and they hurry and they fuss and they fret
They waste your nights and days
Them, I will forget
You, I'll remember always
It's a cold black night and it's midsummer's eve
And the stars are spinning around
I still find it so hard to believe

That someone would kick me when I'm down

Meet me at the bottom, don't lag behind
Bring me my boots and shoes
You can hang back or fight your best on the front line
Sing a little bit of these workingman's blues

I'll be back home in a month or two
When the frost is on the vine
I'll punch my spear right straight through
Half-ways down your spine
I'll lift up my arms to the starry skies
And pray the fugitive's prayer
I'm guessing tomorrow the sun will rise
I hope the final judgment's fair

The battle is over up in the hills
And the mist is closing in
Look at me, with all of my spoils
What did I ever win?
Gotta brand new suit and a brand new wife
I can live on rice and beans
Some people never worked a day in their life
They don't know what work even means

Meet me at the bottom, don't lag behind
Bring me my boots and shoes
You can hang back or fight your best on the front line
Sing a little bit of these workingman's blues

地平线之外

地平线之外，太阳背后

彩虹尽头，人生刚刚开启

星尘之下，悠长的暮色里

地平线之外，容易相爱

我凝望着一个古镇

的窗外

花瓣从花朵

跌落于地

地平线之外，春天或秋季

爱会永远等待，一人或全体

地平线之外，穿过差异

午夜时分，我们会在同一战壕

山涧流水，已然变冷

地平线之外，有人在为你的灵魂祈祷

我失去了我的真爱

在黄昏，在晨曦

我必须恢复

起来，继续

地平线之外，超越燃烧的爱

你每走一步，我亦步亦趋

地平线之外，夜风吹拂
来自很久以前的旋律主题
圣玛丽的钟声，敲得多甜蜜
地平线之外，我及时找到了你
滑行，失足
来不及止步
滑翔，漂浮
高处不胜寒
地平线之外，天空如此蔚蓝
我不止一辈子可以爱你

Beyond the Horizon

Beyond the horizon, behind the sun
At the end of the rainbow life has only begun
In the long hours of twilight 'neath the stardust above
Beyond the horizon it is easy to love
I'm staring out the window
Of an ancient town
Petals from flowers
Falling to the ground
Beyond the horizon, in the springtime or fall
Love waits forever, for one and for all

Beyond the horizon, across the divide
'Round about midnight, we'll be on the same side
Down in the valley the water runs cold
Beyond the horizon someone's prayin' for your soul
I lost my true lover
In the dusk, in the dawn
I have to recover
Get up and go on
Beyond the horizon, beyond love's burning game
Every step that you take, I'm walking the same

Beyond the horizon, the night winds blow
The theme of a melody from many moons ago
The bells of St. Mary, how sweetly they chime
Beyond the horizon I found you just in time
Slipping and sliding
Too late to stop
Riding and gliding

It's lonely at the top
Beyond the horizon, the sky is so blue
I've got more than a lifetime to live lovin' you

内蒂·摩尔

迷惘的约翰坐在铁轨上
有哪儿不对劲
早上蓝调像冰雹般落下
留下一串油腻腻的痕迹

我将周游世界
然后回来看你
我除了拼搏就是奋斗
如果没有人被我伤害，我会活着回来

我是一个疯子的长子
在一支牛仔乐队里
有一堆罪要偿，没时间躲藏
如果我知道你在另一边，亲爱的，我会穿越烈焰

噢，我想你，内蒂·摩尔
我的幸福已经收场
冬天走了，河水上涨
我爱你，一如既往
但这儿已无人可以诉说

我的眼前漆黑一片

研究领域变得疯狂

太多的文书工作

阿尔伯特在墓堆，弗兰姬大吵大嚷 [1]

我开始相信《圣经》中的教诲

我要去"南方"与"黄狗"的交会点 [2]

远离所有这些煽动者

这些倒霉女人像胶水一样黏人

非此即彼或两者皆非

她说："爸爸，小心，别把裤子撕裂。

这场舞会上你会喝废。"

他们说威士忌会杀了你，但我不觉得

我和你一起驾车去山巅

---

1. 指涉美国传统歌曲《弗兰姬与阿尔伯特》（*Frankie and Albert*），此歌讲述了弗兰姬发现阿尔伯特出轨而将他枪杀的故事。

2. 南方，指南方铁路；黄狗，是亚祖三角洲铁路的昵称。两条铁路历史上曾在密西西比州穆尔黑德（Moorhead）交会，据传 1903 年蓝调之父汉迪（W. C. Handy）在此地听到一位老人演唱《南方与黄狗交会的地方》（*Where the Southern Cross the Dog*），后来在此基础上创作了早期蓝调歌曲《黄狗蓝调》（*Yellow Dog Blues*）。南方与黄狗的交会点于是成了蓝调音乐史上的重要地点。

噢，我想你，内蒂·摩尔

我的幸福已经收场

冬天走了，河水上涨

我爱你，一如既往

但这儿已无人可以诉说

我的眼前漆黑一片

不知道为什么，我的宝贝儿从没那么好看过

我不必再疑惑

她整天都在做饭，我吃掉她得花上整晚

我一口吃不下那么多

法官入内，全体起立

抬起你的眼

你可以为所欲为，你不需要我的意见

在你辱骂我之前，你最好考虑再三

天亮了，温降了

我想雨已经停了

我要让你去直面命运

当我收拾完你，你会明白要管好你自己

噢，我想你，内蒂·摩尔

我的幸福已经收场

冬天走了，河水上涨

我爱你，一如既往

但这儿已无人可以诉说

我的眼前漆黑一片

稳定的灯光闪着火花

模糊了我的视线

当你在我身旁，我的悲伤一扫而光

和你过一辈子就像活在天堂

我以为对的，都被证明是错的

我将随波漂荡

我心爱的女人，主宰着我的心

没有刀能斩断我们的爱情

今天我要虔诚站起，提高

赞美的音量 [1]

阳光强烈，我站在光里

衷心希望这是晚上

1.《旧约·历代志下》5:13：“用各种乐器，扬声赞美耶和华说⋯⋯”

噢，我想你，内蒂·摩尔

我的幸福已经收场

冬天走了，河水上涨

我爱你，一如既往

但这儿已无人可以诉说

我的眼前漆黑一片

Nettie Moore

Lost John sittin' on a railroad track
Something's out of whack
Blues this morning falling down like hail
Gonna leave a greasy trail

Gonna travel the world is what I'm gonna do
Then come back and see you
All I ever do is struggle and strive
If I don't do anybody any harm, I might make it back home
    alive

I'm the oldest son of a crazy man
I'm in a cowboy band
Got a pile of sins to pay for and I ain't got time to hide
I'd walk through a blazing fire, baby, if I knew you was on
    the other side

Oh, I miss you Nettie Moore
And my happiness is o'er
Winter's gone, the river's on the rise
I loved you then and ever shall
But there's no one here that's left to tell
The world has gone black before my eyes

The world of research has gone berserk
Too much paperwork
Albert's in the graveyard, Frankie's raising hell
I'm beginning to believe what the scriptures tell

I'm going where the Southern crosses the Yellow Dog
Get away from all these demagogues
And these bad luck women stick like glue
It's either one or the other or neither of the two

She says, "Look out daddy, don't want you to tear your
    pants.
You can get wrecked in this dance."
They say whiskey will kill ya, but I don't think it will
I'm riding with you to the top of the hill

Oh, I miss you Nettie Moore
And my happiness is o'er
Winter's gone, the river's on the rise
I loved you then and ever shall
But there's no one here that's left to tell
The world has gone black before my eyes

Don't know why my baby never looked so good before
I don't have to wonder no more
She been cooking all day and it's gonna take me all night
I can't eat all that stuff in a single bite

The Judge is coming in, everybody rise
Lift up your eyes
You can do what you please, you don't need my advice
Before you call me any dirty names you better think twice

Getting light outside, the temperature dropped
I think the rain has stopped
I'm going to make you come to grips with fate
When I'm through with you, you'll learn to keep your
    business straight

Oh, I miss you Nettie Moore
And my happiness is o'er
Winter's gone, the river's on the rise
I loved you then and ever shall
But there's no one here that's left to tell
The world has gone black before my eyes

The bright spark of the steady lights
Has dimmed my sights
When you're around all my grief gives 'way
A lifetime with you is like some heavenly day

Everything I've ever known to be right has been proven
    wrong
I'll be drifting along
The woman I'm lovin', she rules my heart
No knife could ever cut our love apart

Today I'll stand in faith and raise
The voice of praise
The sun is strong, I'm standing in the light
I wish to God that it were night

Oh, I miss you Nettie Moore
And my happiness is o'er
Winter's gone, the river's on the rise
I loved you then and ever shall
But there's no one here that's left to tell
The world has gone black before my eyes

大堤将决

如果雨下个不停，大堤就会决口 [1]
如果雨下个不停，大堤就会决口
大家都说这鬼天只有上帝造得出

哦，我在大堤上劳作，妈妈，不分黑夜白昼
哦，我在大堤上劳作，妈妈，不分黑夜白昼
我来到河边，扔掉我的衣服

我服完了刑，现在我完好如新
我服完了刑，现在我完好如新
他们不能把我抓回去，除非我要他们把我抓走

如果雨下个不停，大堤就会决口
如果雨下个不停，大堤就会决口
这些人要剥夺你的所有

---

1. 源自美国蓝调夫妻歌手"堪萨斯"乔·麦考伊（Kansas Joe McCoy）
与"孟菲斯"米妮（Memphis Minnie）的歌曲《当大堤决口》（*When the Levee Breaks*），原歌词取材自 1927 年密西西比大洪灾。

我不能在这儿落脚，我还没准备好卸下心中的石头
我不能在这儿落脚，我还没准备好卸下心中的石头
财富和救赎会在下一个弯道守候

我把你救出阴沟，这就是我得到的谢意
我把你救出阴沟，这就是我得到的谢意
你说希望我戒掉你，我说不，还没到时候

我看着你的眼睛，里面除了我谁都没有
我看着你的眼睛，里面除去我谁都没有
我看到了我的所有，和我希望成为的所有

如果雨下个不停，大堤就会决口
如果雨下个不停，大堤就会决口
这些人不知道选择哪条路走

当我和你在一起，我忘了我忧郁过
当我和你在一起，我忘了我忧郁过
没有你，我做什么都没意义

有些人在路上，携带着全部家当
有些人在路上，携带着全部家当
有些人几乎没有，足够的皮来包骨头

穿上你的猫服，妈妈，穿上你的晚礼服

穿上你的猫服，妈妈，穿上你的晚礼服

再苦个几年，就有一千年的幸福

如果雨下个不停，大堤就会决口

如果雨下个不停，大堤就会决口

我曾试着让你爱上我，但我不会一错再错

如果雨下个不停，大堤就会决口

如果雨下个不停，大堤就会决口

还有许多便宜货等着拿走

我早上醒来，床上有鸡蛋和黄油

我早上醒来，床上有鸡蛋和黄油

我连抬头的地儿都没有

回来吧，亲爱的，说我们不会再分手

回来吧，亲爱的，说我们不会再分手

别没脑没心，形同陌路

如果雨下个不停，大堤就会决口

如果雨下个不停，大堤就会决口

有人还在梦境，有人睡意全无

The Levee's Gonna Break

If it keep on rainin' the levee gonna break
If it keep on rainin' the levee gonna break
Everybody saying this is a day only the Lord could make

Well I worked on the levee Mama, both night and day
Well I worked on the levee Mama, both night and day
I got to the river and I threw my clothes away

I paid my time and now I'm as good as new
I paid my time and now I'm as good as new
They can't take me back, not unless I want them to

If it keep on rainin' the levee gonna break
If it keep on rainin' the levee gonna break
Some of these people gonna strip you of all they can take

I can't stop here, I ain't ready to unload
I can't stop here, I ain't ready to unload
Riches and salvation can be waiting behind the next bend in
    the road

I picked you up from the gutter and this is the thanks I get
I picked you up from the gutter and this is the thanks I get
You say you want me to quit ya, I told you no, not just yet

I look in your eyes, I see nobody else but me
I look in your eyes, I see nobody other than me
I see all that I am and all I hope to be

If it keep on rainin' the levee gonna break
If it keep on rainin' the levee gonna break
Some of these people don't know which road to take

When I'm with you I forget I was ever blue
When I'm with you I forget I was ever blue
Without you there's no meaning in anything I do

Some people on the road carrying everything that they own
Some people on the road carrying everything that they own
Some people got barely enough skin to cover their bones

Put on your cat clothes, Mama, put on your evening dress
Put on your cat clothes, Mama, put on your evening dress
A few more years of hard work then there'll be a thousand
    years of happiness

If it keep on rainin' the levee gonna break
If it keep on rainin' the levee gonna break
I tried to get you to love me, but I won't repeat that mistake

If it keep on rainin' the levee gonna break
If it keep on rainin' the levee gonna break
Plenty of cheap stuff out there still around to take

I woke up this morning, butter and eggs in my bed
I woke up this morning, butter and eggs in my bed
I ain't got enough room to even raise my head

Come back, baby, say we never more will part
Come back, baby, say we never more will part
Don't be a stranger without a brain or heart

If it keep on rainin' the levee gonna break
If it keep on rainin' the levee gonna break
Some people still sleepin', some people are wide awake

沉默是金

我走在今晚的神秘花园
伤花从藤上垂下
我走过凉快的水晶喷泉
有人从后面给我一拳

沉默是金，只是前行
穿过这令人厌倦的悲哀世界
心在燃烧，依然憧憬
世上无人知情

他们说祈祷管用
所以妈妈为我祈祷吧
人们的心里住着一个恶魔
我努力去爱邻舍，善待他人
但是妈妈，并非一帆风顺

沉默是金，只是前行
我要在你过桥前烧掉那座桥
心在燃烧，依然憧憬
你一旦输了没人怜悯

我被哭哭啼啼搞得意志消沉

我满眼噙泪，口干舌燥

如果敌人酣睡时被我撞到

我会在他们的栖身之地举起屠刀

沉默是金，只是前行

穿过这模糊不清的神秘世界

心在燃烧，依然憧憬

走过瘟疫之城

这世界充满了臆想

这个广阔的人们说是圆形的世界

他们会把你的心从沉思中拉走

在你沮丧时给你雪上加霜

沉默是金，只是前行

在猪眼镇里吃猪眼油脂

心在燃烧，依然憧憬

总有一天你会庆幸有我在左右

他们会用钱和权压垮你

醒着的每一刻你都可能垮掉

我会充分利用最后一个钟头

报杀父之仇，然后退后

沉默是金，只是前行
把我的拐杖递来
心在燃烧，依然憧憬
得把你从我痛苦的脑海里赶走

天堂明亮，时轮飞转
声名和荣耀好像永不失色
火焰虽灭，光亮永驻
谁说我得不到上天眷顾？

沉默是金，只是前行
手持一个死人的盾牌
心在燃烧，依然憧憬
忍着脚跟的牙疼前进

痛楚无穷无尽
每个角落都渗着泪水
我没在演，我没在装
我没心怀多余的恐惧

沉默是金，只是前行

从那夜走到现在
心在燃烧，依然憧憬
直走到视野之外

我走在神秘花园
在一个炎热的夏日，一个炎热夏日的草坪上
对不起，夫人，请原谅
这里空无一人，园丁已经离开

沉默是金，只是前行
沿路走，过弯道
心在燃烧，依然憧憬
在最后的内陆，在世界的尽头

Ain't Talkin'

As I walked out tonight in the mystic garden
The wounded flowers were dangling from the vines
I was passing by yon cool and crystal fountain
Someone hit me from behind

Ain't talkin', just walkin'
Through this weary world of woe
Heart burnin', still yearnin'
No one on earth would ever know

They say prayer has the power to help
So pray for me mother
In the human heart an evil spirit can dwell
I'm trying to love my neighbor and do good unto others
But oh, mother, things ain't going well

Ain't talkin', just walkin'
I'll burn that bridge before you can cross
Heart burnin', still yearnin'
They'll be no mercy for you once you've lost

Now I'm all worn down by weepin'
My eyes are filled with tears, my lips are dry
If I catch my opponents ever sleepin'
I'll just slaughter them where they lie

Ain't talkin', just walkin'
Through a world mysterious and vague
Heart burnin', still yearnin'

Walking through the cities of the plague

The whole world is filled with speculation
The whole wide world which people say is round
They will tear your mind away from contemplation
They will jump on your misfortune when you're down

Ain't talkin', just walkin'
Eatin' hog-eyed grease in hog-eyed town
Heart burnin', still yearnin'
Someday you'll be glad to have me around

They will crush you with wealth and power
Every waking moment you could crack
I'll make the most of one last extra hour
I'll avenge my father's death then I'll step back

Ain't talkin', just walkin'
Hand me down my walkin' cane
Heart burnin', still yearnin'
Got to get you out of my miserable brain

It's bright in the heavens and the wheels are flying
Fame and honor never seem to fade
The fire's gone out but the light is never dying
Who says I can't get heavenly aid?

Ain't talkin', just walkin'
Carrying a dead man's shield
Heart burnin', still yearnin'
Walkin' with a toothache in my heel

The suffering is unending

Every nook and cranny has its tears
I'm not playing, I'm not pretending
I'm not nursing any superfluous fears

Ain't talkin', just walkin'
Walkin' ever since the other night
Heart burnin', still yearnin'
Walkin' 'til I'm clean out of sight

As I walked out in the mystic garden
On a hot summer day, hot summer lawn
Excuse me, ma'am, I beg your pardon
There's no one here, the gardener is gone

Ain't talkin', just walkin'
Up the road around the bend
Heart burnin', still yearnin'
In the last outback, at the world's end

逃不开你

哦，夜车滚滚向前
沿着归家的路
我的所有希望已露端倪
我的所有梦想已入歧途
山坡渐渐变暗
星星从天而降
尘世欢愉尽皆消散
夜晚未被爱情改变
这张灰色的天幕下
我会一直待到明天
假装不再悲伤
我的心飘在远方
死亡钟声正在鸣响
我的列车已经晚点
我紧紧抓住你的回忆
我逃不开你

哦，我听到雷声轰鸣
响亮而悠长
有时你一定困惑

上帝知道我没做错

你浪费了你所有的力量

扔掉了圣诞派

你会像花朵一样凋落

装傻逗笑，撒手人寰

我不悲伤也不遗憾

我一身黑色盛装

为声名和荣耀而战

你试图让我拼命苦干

在遥远的乐土

太阳破云而出

我们本该一起走过

我逃不开你

我抓不住影子

它们聚在门边

雨水倾落窗前

真想多看你几眼

前路永远蜿蜒

星辰永不朽迈

晨光令人目眩

世界是个舞台

应是欢愉时光

四处都是欢颜
但疯狂的谜团
却在空中播散
我不喜欢这座城
不像有些人
我逃不开你
这难道不遗憾?

Can't Escape from You

Oh the evening train is rolling
All along the homeward way
All my hopes are over the horizon
All my dreams have gone astray
The hillside darkly shaded
Stars fall from above
All the joys of earth have faded
The nights untouched by love
I'll be here 'til tomorrow
Beneath a shroud of gray
I'll pretend I'm free from sorrow
My heart is miles away
The dead bells are ringing
My train is overdue
To your memory I'm clinging
I can't escape from you

Well I hear the sound of thunder
Roaring loud and long
Sometimes you've got to wonder
God knows I've done no wrong
You've wasted all your power
You threw out the Christmas pie
You'll wither like a flower
And play the fool and die
I'm neither sad nor sorry
I'm all dressed up in black
I fought for fame and glory
You tried to break my back

In the far off sweet forever
The sunshine breaking through
We should have walked together
I can't escape from you

I cannot grasp the shadows
That gather near the door
Rain fall 'round my window
I wish I'd seen you more
The path is ever winding
The stars they never age
The morning light is blinding
All the world's a stage
Should be the time of gladness
Happy faces everywhere
But the mystery of madness
Is propagating in the air
I don't like the city
Not like some folks do
Isn't it a pity
I can't escape from you?

哈克之歌 [1]

哦，我独自游荡

穿过一片戈壁

梦见未来妻子

我仗剑在手

接过重担

征战死亡人生

我的盘子和杯子

摆放整齐

我从一个孩子手里拿了枝玫瑰

当我吻你的唇

甜蜜直往下滴

但我不得不暂时收手

我们每天邂逅

在任何老街

你正值豆蔻

高矮肥瘦

---

1. 迪伦为美国电影《幸运赌神》（*Lucky You*，2007）所作的歌曲，哈克即片中男主角，是一位技术高超的职业赌徒。

都来参加舞会

我每场都到

每一棵树背后

都有东西可看

这条河不止一英里宽

我们恋过两回

你对我不好

我不得不暂时收手

护士来了

她包里有钱

女士们先生们来了

你押上了所有

你没机会赢

你一直搏到最后

我躺在沙滩上

晒成健康色

驾车拉风前行

你把我迷倒

从脚到头

我不得不暂时收手

我数着时光

一滴泪都没有淌

看不清原本会怎样

大自然之声

叫我心欢喜

给我放着狂野的风之歌

我找到了无望的爱情

在楼上的房间

在日暖风和的一天

你醇美如酒

我没在骗你

但我不得不暂时收手

所有快乐的小精灵

会上吊自尽

我的信仰冷酷到底

我的钱堆积如山

我不是没有证据

如果你不相信，就来看一看

你觉得我伤感

我也这么想

用我的话来讲，看不到出老千

游戏已老旧

纸牌已凉透

而我不得不暂时收手

游戏已老旧
纸牌已凉透
我不得不暂时收手

Huck's Tune

Well I wandered alone
Through a desert of stone
And I dreamt of my future wife
My sword's in my hand
And I'm next in command
In this version of death called life
My plate and my cup
Are right straight up
I took a rose from the hand of a child
When I kiss your lips
The honey drips
But I'm gonna have to put you down for a while

Every day we meet
On any old street
And you're in your girlish prime
The short and the tall
Are coming to the ball
I go there all the time
Behind every tree
There's something to see
The river is wider than a mile
I tried you twice
You couldn't be nice
I'm gonna have to put you down for a while

Here come the nurse
With money in her purse
Here come the ladies and men

You push it all in
And you've no chance to win
You play 'em on down to the end
I'm laying in the sand
Getting a sunshine tan
Moving along, riding in style
From my toes to my head
You knock me dead
I'm gonna have to put you down for a while

I count the years
And I shed no tears
I'm blinded to what might have been
Nature's voice
Makes my heart rejoice
Play me the wild song of the wind
I found hopeless love
In the room above
When the sun and the weather were mild
You're as fine as wine
I ain't handing you no line
But I'm gonna have to put you down for a while

All the merry little elves
Can go hang themselves
My faith is as cold as can be
I'm stacked high to the roof
And I'm not without proof
If you don't believe me, come see
You think I'm blue
I think so too
In my words, you'll find no guile
The game's gotten old

The deck's gone cold
And I'm gonna have to put you down for a while

The game's gotten old
The deck's gone cold
I'm gonna have to put you down for a while

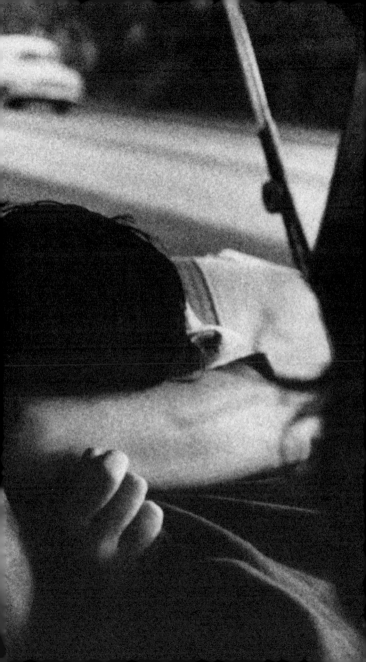

Life is for Love — all they say but Comes Blind
If you want to live Easy, baby — mine —

What the use of all my dreaming / I must have all the
You know dreaming wouldn't do for me anymore

You just as wonderful as Ever — baby you cant start
I must losing my mind

(Pleading) James Joyce (Fan
People —

Everybody put all the money / Buy beautiful clothes
Everybody got flower / but even a single rose

共度此生
Together Through Life

李皖　译（郝佳　校）

《共度此生》是鲍勃·迪伦的第三十三张录音室专辑，发行于 2009 年 4 月 28 日，面世一周便"空降"为包括美、英在内多个国家的排行榜冠军。

此专辑中的歌曲以异常苍老的声音演唱，采用了今天已经基本被弃用的演奏方式，歌词也透着沧桑之感，听起来像是至少半个世纪以前的作品。作为歌手，迪伦仿佛一出生即老去，阅尽世事，此专辑更是覆盖了迪伦自身的层层岁月：既绝望，又火热；既已白发苍苍，又燃起了末路、末世的熊熊涅槃之火。

我曾经用"道成肉身"来评价迪伦的后期作品。作为时代人物，他把自己活成了他最具代表性的作品。他所历经的一个个非凡的年代，都构成了他晚年写作的幽深背景。哪怕只是一首短歌，也由此具有了非同一般的长度、厚度、复杂性与重量，就像他的一生一样意味深长。

此专辑共收录了迪伦的十首作品，其中九首的歌词均是与感恩而死乐队（The Grateful Dead）的词作者罗伯特·亨特（Robert Hunter）共同创作。在这些歌词里，迪伦重新采用了民歌史上那些老歌的样式，诉说着既像包围着他现在、又像缠绕着他一生的感受。他感到了周围的世界充满了欺骗、丑恶与危险，隐隐有种说不出的预兆，境况似乎越变越坏。从中，你能听到这位老人的失望与悲哀，他好像历经了劫难，已精疲力竭。但在这黑暗的声音中仍有着一丝温存，里面的情歌，仍然是火热的。

李皖

在此之外，一无所有

（与罗伯特·亨特合作）

我爱你，漂亮宝贝

你是我知道的，唯一的爱

只要你在陪伴我

全世界就是我的王座

在此之外，一无所有

再没有什么能宣称为我们所有

这是后半夜

我在满是破车的街道走着

不知道没有了这宣称是属于我们的爱

我还能干什么

在此之外，一无所有

除了这星星和明月

每条大街都有一扇窗

每一扇窗都是玻璃做的

我们将爱下去，漂亮宝贝

一直爱到爱能持续的最后

在此之外，一无所有
除了那过去年岁的连绵山岳

我的船在海港
帆已张起就要启航
听我说，漂亮宝贝
请把手放在我头上
在此之外，一无所有
什么都没做，什么也都未讲

Beyond Here Lies Nothin'
(with Robert Hunter)

I love you pretty baby
You're the only love I've ever known
Just as long as you stay with me
The whole world is my throne
Beyond here lies nothin'
Nothin' we can call our own

I'm movin' after midnight
Down boulevards of broken cars
Don't know what I'd do without it
Without this love that we call ours
Beyond here lies nothin'
Nothin' but the moon and stars

Down every street there's a window
And every window made of glass
We'll keep on lovin' pretty baby
For as long as love will last
Beyond here lies nothin'
But the mountains of the past

My ship is in the harbor
And the sails are spread
Listen to me pretty baby
Lay your hand upon my head
Beyond here lies nothin'
Nothin' done and nothin' said

人世维艰 [1]

（与罗伯特·亨特合作）

夜风沉寂

道路和意愿已失

我说不上来它们去了哪儿

只体会到这其中含义

一直都小心翼翼

无奈接受着这人世维艰

没有你在身边

你曾经是这样一个朋友

与我这么近，这么亲密

不知不觉却悄悄远离

是在哪儿，我们步入了岔路

我走过那昔日的校园

无奈接受着这人世维艰

没有你在身边

---

1. 迪伦为美法联合制作的公路电影《我自己的情歌》（*My Own Love Song*，2010）而作的歌曲。

从那一天

从你走的那一天

我感到空虚如此广阔

我不知道孰是孰非

只知道我需要力量去反击

反击这外面的世界

自从我们失去了联系

我不再有太多感觉

萧索日甚一日

心已遭到禁闭

我在林阴大道走着

无奈接受着这人世维艰

没有你在身边

太阳渐渐平西

已经是时候离去

我感到一股冷风

取代了记忆

梦锁上，关好了围栏

我无奈接受着这人世维艰

没有你在身边

Life Is Hard
(with Robert Hunter)

The evening winds are still
I've lost the way and will
Can't tell you where they went
I just know what they meant
I'm always on my guard
Admitting life is hard
Without you near me

The friend you used to be
So near and dear to me
You slipped so far away
Where did we go astray
I pass the old schoolyard
Admitting life is hard
Without you near me

Ever since the day
The day you went away
I felt that emptiness so wide
I don't know what's wrong or right
I just know I need strength to fight
Strength to fight that world outside

Since we've been out of touch
I haven't felt that much
From day to barren day
My heart stays locked away

I walk the boulevard
Admitting life is hard
Without you near me

The sun is sinking low
I guess it's time to go
I feel a chilly breeze
In place of memories
My dreams are locked and barred
Admitting life is hard
Without you near me

我老婆的家乡

（与罗伯特·亨特合作）

哦我来这儿不是处理什么狗屁事儿

我来这儿是为了听那鼓手的铙钹响

你甭想让我不开心

我只想说这可是他妈的我老婆的家乡

哦这个有理那个有理

我现在想不起来，但我知道它们在

我坐在阳光中直到皮肤晒成棕色

我只想说这可是他妈的我老婆的家乡

家乡，家乡

她能让你偷，她能让你抢

能给你荨麻疹，让你丢掉工作

让事情变糟，能让事情变更糟

她有那本事比吉普赛咒语更强

终有一天我会逃走

我非常非常确定，她会让我杀人

我将走进去，摇下百叶窗
我只想说这可是他妈的我老婆的家乡

哦太多需要记忆，太多需要忘记
我还能记起我们相遇的日子
很久以前我便失去了理智
我对她的爱是我所知道的一切

州已破碎，县已干涸
别用那恶眼盯着我
往前走好了，不要再磨蹭
我再说一次，这可是他妈的我老婆的家乡
家乡，家乡

My Wife's Home Town
(with Robert Hunter)

Well I didn't come here to deal with a doggone thing
I just came here to hear the drummer's cymbal ring
There ain't no way you can put me down
I just want to say that Hell's my wife's home town

Well there's reasons for that and reasons for this
I can't think of any just now, but I know they exist
I'm sitting in the sun 'til my skin turns brown
I just want to say that Hell's my wife's home town
Home town, home town

She can make you steal, make you rob
Give you the hives, make you lose your job
Make things bad, she can make things worse
She got stuff more potent than a gypsy curse

One of these days, I'll end up on the run
I'm pretty sure, she'll make me kill someone
I'm going inside, roll the shutters down
I just want to say that Hell's my wife's home town

Well there's plenty to remember, plenty to forget
I still can remember the day we met
I lost my reason long ago
My love for her is all I know

State gone broke, the county's dry

Don't be looking at me with that evil eye
Keep on walking, don't be hanging around
I'm telling you again that Hell's my wife's home town
Home town, home town

假如有天你去休斯顿

（与罗伯特·亨特合作）

假如有天你去休斯顿

最好乖乖走路

手插在口袋里

枪带系紧

你会惹上大麻烦

假如你想干仗

假如有天你去休斯顿

小子，你最好乖乖走路

假如有天你去了那里

去了巴格比和拉马尔

你最好当心那个

佩戴着亮星的男人

最好明白你是要去哪儿

或者待在原地

假如有天你去了那里

去了巴格比和拉马尔

我认识这些街道

我以前来过这里

我差点儿在这儿挂掉

在墨西哥战争时期

有些什么总这样

让我一次次地回来

我认识这些街道

我以前来过这里

假如有天你去达拉斯

向玛丽·安妮问声好

说我仍然紧扣着扳机

尽最大可能活下去

如果你见到她姐姐露西

说我很抱歉没在那里

告诉另一个姐姐贝齐

要她去做悔罪的祷告

我得了热病，辗转不宁

脑子里烧着

必须一直往前

再不能去坏事儿

我怎么从这里出去的

就会怎么再回来

我得了热病，辗转不宁

脑子里烧着

假如有天你去奥斯汀

到沃思堡或者圣安东

去找一找那些我迷失过的酒吧

把我的记忆送回家

把我的眼泪装进瓶

拧紧盖子

假如有天你去休斯顿

你最好乖乖走路

If You Ever Go to Houston
(with Robert Hunter)

If you ever go to Houston
Better walk right
Keep your hands in your pockets
And your gun-belt tight
You'll be asking for trouble
If you're lookin' for a fight
If you ever go to Houston
Boy, you better walk right

If you're ever down there
On Bagby and Lamar
You better watch out for
The man with the shining star
Better know where you're going
Or stay where you are
If you're ever down there
On Bagby and Lamar

I know these streets
I've been here before
I nearly got killed here
During the Mexican war
Something always
Keeps me coming back for more
I know these streets
I've been here before

If you ever go to Dallas
Say hello to Mary Anne
Say I'm still pullin' on the trigger
Hangin' on the best that I can
If you see her sister Lucy
Say I'm sorry I'm not there
Tell her other sister Betsy
To pray the sinner's prayer

I got a restless fever
Burnin' in my brain
Got to keep ridin' forward
Can't spoil the game
The same way I leave here
Will be the way that I came
Got a restless fever
Burnin' in my brain

If you ever go to Austin
Fort Worth or San Antone
Find the bar rooms I got lost in
And send my memories home
Put my tears in a bottle
Screw the top on tight
If you ever go to Houston
You better walk right

健忘的心

（与罗伯特·亨特合作）

健忘的心

失去了回忆的力量

那每一个小细节

无从再想

对我们俩的岁月

谁会比你记得更多

健忘的心

你和我，那美好时光，我们笑着

那已经是很久以前

你现在满足于让一天天流过

只要你在那儿

就是我祈祷的应允

健忘的心

生命能赐予的爱，我们都爱过了

我能说什么呢

没有你日子太难过

再也再也无法承受

为什么我们不能像从前一样相爱

健忘的心

仿佛脑海中一片行走的暗影

整夜整夜

我醒着听那疼痛的声音

门永远地关上了

如果真的，曾经有过一扇门

Forgetful Heart
(with Robert Hunter)

Forgetful heart
Lost your power of recall
Every little detail
You don't remember at all
The times we knew
Who would remember better than you

Forgetful heart
We laughed and had a good time, you and I
It's been so long
Now you're content to let the days go by
When you were there
You were the answer to my prayer

Forgetful heart
We loved with all the love that life can give
What can I say
Without you it's so hard to live
Can't take much more
Why can't we love like we did before

Forgetful heart
Like a walking shadow in my brain
All night long
I lay awake and listen to the sound of pain
The door has closed forevermore
If indeed there ever was a door

茱莲妮

（与罗伯特·亨特合作）

哦，你沿着繁华大街走来，走在那阳光下
你让死人复活，大喊着"她就是那一个"
茱莲妮，茱莲妮
宝贝啊，我是王，你是那王后

哦，这是条漫长的老旧公路，没有尽头
我有支"周六夜特用"手枪，我回来了
我会睡你门口，把我的一生押上去
你可能对此一无所知，但我会让你属于我
茱莲妮，茱莲妮
宝贝啊，我是王，你是那王后

我把手一直放在兜里，径直向前
人们以为他们知道，但是他们都错了
你是那么可爱，我将抢过我的色子
只要让我做到了一次，我就有第二次
茱莲妮，茱莲妮
宝贝啊，我是王，你是那王后

哦，我知道这得来不易，对此我已经尝透
你看不到那个人，他已没有了退路
那大大的褐色眼珠，放射出一束光焰
这时你用胳膊搂着我，一切再不是那么黑暗
茱莲妮，茱莲妮
宝贝啊，我是王，你是那王后

Jolene
(with Robert Hunter)

Well you're comin' down High Street, walkin' in the sun
You make the dead man rise and holler she's the one
Jolene, Jolene
Baby, I am the king and you're the queen

Well it's a long old highway, don't ever end
I've got a Saturday night special, I'm back again
I'll sleep by your door, lay my life on the line
You probably don't know, but I'm gonna make you mine
Jolene, Jolene
Baby, I am the king and you're the queen

I keep my hands in my pocket, I'm movin' along
People think they know, but they're all wrong
You're something nice, I'm gonna grab my dice
If I can do it once, I can do it twice
Jolene, Jolene
Baby, I am the king and you're the queen

Well I found out the hard way, I've had my fill
You can't find somebody with his back to a hill
Those big brown eyes, they set off a spark
When you hold me in your arms things don't look so dark
Jolene, Jolene
Baby, I am the king and you're the queen

关于你的这个梦

在这乌有之乡的咖啡馆我能待多久
当那黑夜尚未变成白昼
我在想为何我是如此害怕天明
所有我所有，所有我所知
是关于你的这个梦
是它让我活下去

存在着这么一刻，所有的老朽
都再次新生
但是这一刻，想必来了又失去
所有我所有，所有我所知
是关于你的这个梦
是它让我活下去

我望向别处，但还是看见
我不想相信，但一直还在相信
影子们在墙上跳舞
那似乎什么都知道的影子

是我太瞎吗，所以看不见？

是我的心一直在耍我吗？

罢手已太晚，纵使朋友们都已离去

所有我所有，所有我所知

是关于你的这个梦

是它让我活下去

我能触摸到的一切，似乎在消失

无论我转向哪里，你一直都在这里

我将继续这场赛跑直到尘世生命终结

我将保卫这地方用我那垂死的呼吸

从帘布沉沉的郁闷屋子

我看见一颗星从天上坠落

等我转头再看，它已消失不见

所有我所有，所有我所知

是关于你的这个梦

是它让我活下去

This Dream of You

How long can I stay in this nowhere café
'Fore night turns into day
I wonder why I'm so frightened of dawn
All I have and all I know
Is this dream of you
Which keeps me living on

There's a moment when all old things
Become new again
But that moment might have been here and gone
All I have and all I know
Is this dream of you
Which keeps me living on

I look away, but I keep seeing it
I don't want to believe, but I keep believing it
Shadows dance upon the wall
Shadows that seem to know it all

Am I too blind to see?
Is my heart playing tricks on me?
Too late to stop now even though all my friends are gone
All I have and all I know
Is this dream of you
Which keeps me living on

Everything I touch seems to disappear
Everywhere I turn you are always here
I'll run this race until my earthly death

I'll defend this place with my dying breath

From a cheerless room in a curtained gloom
I saw a star from heaven fall
I turned and looked again but it was gone
All I have and all I know
Is this dream of you
Which keeps me living on

摇一摇妈妈 [1]

（与罗伯特·亨特合作）

你让我郁郁不乐宝贝当我抬头看着太阳

你让我郁郁不乐宝贝当我抬头看着太阳

回到这儿来吧我们来真正地乐一场

哦入夜还不久一切都很平静

哦入夜还不久一切都很平静

再一次，我在攀登那心碎山的山顶

摇一摇，摇一摇妈妈，像一艘船要出海去

摇一摇，摇一摇妈妈，像一艘船要出海去

你拿光了我的钱，把它全给了理查德·李

沿着那河岸辛普森法官在踱步

沿着那河岸辛普森法官在踱步

没谁比那个老小丑，更让我震惊不已

---

1. 妈妈，口语中又有"情人""妻子"之意。

你们有些女人真的明白了自己是什么东西
你们有些女人真的明白了自己是什么东西
但你们的衣服全破了你们的语言有点儿粗鄙

摇一摇，摇一摇妈妈，摇一摇直到天破晓
摇一摇，摇一摇妈妈，摇一摇直到天破晓
我就在这儿宝贝儿，我并没有走掉

我无母、无父，也几乎无朋友
我无母、无父，也几乎无朋友
这是星期五的早上在富兰克林大道

摇一摇，摇一摇妈妈，提高嗓门儿开始祈祷
摇一摇，摇一摇妈妈，提高嗓门儿开始祈祷
如果你现在回家，最好抄最近的道

Shake Shake Mama
(with Robert Hunter)

I get the blues for you baby when I look up at the sun
I get the blues for you baby when I look up at the sun
Come back here we can have some real fun

Well it's early in the evening and everything is still
Well it's early in the evening and everything is still
One more time, I'm walking up on Heartbreak Hill

Shake, shake mama, like a ship goin' out to sea
Shake, shake mama, like a ship goin' out to sea
You took all my money and you give it to Richard Lee

Down by the river Judge Simpson walkin' around
Down by the river Judge Simpson walkin' around
Nothing shocks me more than that old clown

Some of you women you really know your stuff
Some of you women you really know your stuff
But your clothes are all torn and your language is a little too
    rough

Shake, shake mama, shake it 'til the break of day
Shake, shake mama, shake it 'til the break of day
I'm right here baby, I'm not that far away

I'm motherless, fatherless, almost friendless too
I'm motherless, fatherless, almost friendless too

It's Friday morning on Franklin Avenue

Shake, shake mama, raise your voice and pray
Shake, shake mama, raise your voice and pray
If you're goin' on home, better go the shortest way

我感到一个变化在临近

（与罗伯特·亨特合作）

哦我望遍世界

远望到东方

望见我的小宝贝

和村里的神父一起走来

我感到一个变化在临近

而这一天的最后一部分业已过去

我们有这么多相同之处

我们争取着一样的结局

而我已等不及

等不及我们成为朋友

我感到一个变化在临近

而这一天的第四个部分业已过去

人生是为了爱

而他们说爱是盲目的

如果你想活得轻松

宝贝把你的衣服和我的收拾在一起

我感到一个变化在临近

而这一天的第四个部分业已过去

做梦没什么用

我有更该做的事

做梦从不起作用

哪怕它们真的变成真的

你一如既往地妖冶

这并不令人惊讶

我们看见生活的意义

就在彼此的眼睛里

我感到一个变化在临近

而这一天的第四个部分业已过去

我听着比利·乔·谢弗[1]

我读着詹姆斯·乔伊斯

有一些人告诉我

我的声音里有土地的血

---

1. 比利·乔·谢弗（Billy Joe Shaver, 1939— ），美国得克萨斯乡村音乐
歌手和词作者。

人人有了钱

人人有了漂亮衣服

人人有了花

我甚至没有一枝玫瑰

我感到一个变化在临近

而这一天的第四个部分业已过去

I Feel a Change Comin' On
(with Robert Hunter)

Well I'm looking the world over
Looking far off into the East
And I see my baby coming
She's walking with the village priest
I feel a change coming on
And the last part of the day is already gone

We got so much in common
We strive for the same old ends
And I just can't wait
Wait for us to become friends
I feel a change coming on
And the fourth part of the day is already gone

Life is for love
And they say that love is blind
If you want to live easy
Baby pack your clothes with mine
I feel a change coming on
And the fourth part of the day is already gone

Ain't no use in dreamin'
I got better things to do
Dreams never worked anyway
Even when they did come true

You're as whorish as ever

It ain't no surprise
We see the meaning of life
In each other's eyes
I feel a change coming on
And the fourth part of the day is already gone

I'm hearing Billy Joe Shaver
And I'm reading James Joyce
Some people they tell me
I got the blood of the land in my voice

Everybody got all the money
Everybody got all the beautiful clothes
Everybody got all the flowers
I don't have one single rose
I feel a change coming on
And the fourth part of the day is already gone

一切都好
（与罗伯特·亨特合作）

议论我吧宝贝，如果必须这样
扔来泥巴，堆起灰尘
我只会做一件事，如果我能做
你听见他们说了——他们说一切都好
都好
一切都好

大政客在说谎
餐馆厨房里，满是苍蝇
不要作什么区分，别弄懂为什么这样
我会告诉你一点——一切都好
一切都好
一切都好

妻子们在离开丈夫，开始转悠
她们离开了聚会，也决不回家
我不会作改变，纵使我能做到
同样的老故事——一切都好

一切都好

都好

一块砖接着一块砖，他们把你拆掉

一杯水足以将人淹死

去检查一下油，看看引擎盖下

不管看到什么，一切都好

都好

说一切都好

这国家的人，这土地上的人

有一些病得这么重，几乎站立不住

每个人都想离开，假如他可以

这难以相信，但一切都好

是的

寡妇的叫喊，孤儿的求乞

你望向各处，看到更多痛苦

跟我来宝贝，我希望你乐意

你知道我要说什么，一切都好

都好，我说一切都好

都好

冷血凶手，城中游荡
警车闪耀，罪案滋长
建筑物在附近崩塌
别怀疑，一切都好
一切都好
他们说一切都好

我将拔下你的胡须吹你脸上
明天这时候我将睡在你那地方
我出去一下就回，弄一些柴火
事实就是这样，而一切都好
一切都好

It's All Good
(with Robert Hunter)

Talk about me babe, if you must
Throw on the dirt, pile on the dust
I'd do the same thing if I could
You've heard what they say—they say it's all good
All good
It's all good

Big politician telling lies
Restaurant kitchen, all full of flies
Don't make a bit of difference, don't see why it should
I'll tell ya somethin'—it's all good
It's all good
It's all good

Wives are leavin' their husbands, they beginning to roam
They leave the party and they never get home
I wouldn't change it, even if I could
Same ol' story—it's all good
It's all good
All good

Brick by brick, they tear you down
A teacup of water is enough to drown
Check your oil, look under the hood
Whatever you see, it's all good
All good
Say it's all good

People in the country, people on the land
Some so sick, they can hardly stand
Everybody would move away, if they could
It's hard to believe but it's all good
Yeah

The widow's cry, the orphan's plea
Everywhere you look, more misery
Come 'long with me, babe, I wish you would
You know what I'm sayin', it's all good
All good, I said it's all good
All good

Cold blooded killer, stalking the town
Cop cars blinking, something bad going down
Buildings are crumbling in the neighborhood
No doubt about it, it's all good
It's all good
They say it's all good

I'll pluck off your beard and blow it in your face
This time tomorrow I'll be rolling in your place
I'm going out back, get some firewood
It is what it is, and it's all good
It's all good

5.   Set 'm up Joe, play Walkin' th Floor
It's not like nobody's ever asked you before
with check th lights and you make Amends
while th smile of Heaven descends
If love is a sin then beauty's a crime
All things are beautiful in their time
The black white, th yellow ad browns
It's all right here for you in Scarlet Town

Thn tell me tht
Th Low s the Law
—

— Yur playing I gan   — th... an
my the cells   war lika frou-
just   al vude
yurself

Some forntnlnys
crosses th
Line

punkt th quality
punkd   Vllrgknt
th
schoolboy pings

Thdoors are chained

暴风雨
Tempest

陈震 译

　　2012 年，七十一岁的鲍勃·迪伦还在进行他已持续二十四年的"永无休止"（Never Ending）世界巡演。这一年年初，他把巡演乐队原班人马拉进录音棚，录制了新专辑《暴风雨》。这是迪伦迄今最后一张原创专辑，距他发表处女专辑整整过去了半个世纪。

　　迪伦用他愈发粗砺的破锣嗓唱着拿手的长篇叙事诗。他絮叨着、嘟嚷着、低吼着一个个宏大沉重的故事。这些故事大多骇人，涉及坏女人、性、复仇、谋杀、强盗、死亡、死亡，还是死亡……其中一首沉闷冗长却又听不厌的安魂曲，用三个和弦、十四分钟、四十五段歌词重现了泰坦尼克号沉没的百年悲剧，也贡献了专辑里最多的死亡人数。

　　难怪西方乐评界普遍认为《暴风雨》是迪伦最黑暗的一张专辑。

　　迪伦把结尾曲《前进吧，约翰》（Roll on, John）献给约翰·列侬，向这位已故摇滚巨人致敬。这首歌依然与死亡有关，但又带有奋进的情绪。迪伦在刚出道时，翻唱过一首同名的传统民谣。那时，二十出头的迪伦如饥似渴地从传统中汲取营养，逐渐形成自己的风格。五十年过去了，迪伦就像一块滚动的石头，从未停止向前滚动，也从未停止向传统致敬。这首《前进吧，约翰》也许是隔空唱给另一位摇滚标杆，又也许是唱给他自己。他还在向前滚动。前进吧，鲍勃。

陈震

迪尤肯汽笛

（与罗伯特·亨特合作）

听那迪尤肯汽笛鸣响

鸣得像要把我的世界一扫而光

我要在卡本代尔歇歇脚再继续跑

那班迪尤肯火车将载我昼夜飞驰

你说我是皮条客，你说我是赌鬼

但我两者皆非

听那迪尤肯汽笛鸣响

听起来像退休前的最后一班岗

听那迪尤肯汽笛鸣响

鸣得像她初次开嗓

蓝光忽闪，红光微闪

鸣得像她来到我卧房

你透过篱笆冲我微笑

就像你从前总漾着的微笑

听那迪尤肯汽笛鸣响

鸣得像她再也不会开嗓

你听不到迪尤肯汽笛鸣响吗

鸣得像天空将要爆炸

你是唯一驱我前行的生命

你像埋在我心底的定时炸弹

我听见甜美的嗓音轻轻呼唤

一定是我们主的母亲

听那迪尤肯汽笛鸣响

鸣得像我的女人在车上

听那迪尤肯汽笛鸣响

鸣得像要鸣走我的忧伤

你这老流氓，我晓得你要去哪

天亮时我会带你到那

每天早上醒来，那女人都在我床上

人人都说她进了我的心房

听那迪尤肯汽笛鸣响

鸣得像要杀我一样

你听不到迪尤肯汽笛鸣响吗
鸣过又一个无用的城镇
老家的灯火微微闪亮
不知道下次回来他们还认识我不

不知道那株老橡树是否还在
那株老橡树，我们从前常爬的那一株

听那迪尤肯汽笛鸣响
鸣得像她准时开嗓

Duquesne Whistle
(with Robert Hunter)

Listen to that Duquesne whistle blowin'
Blowin' like it's gonna sweep my world away
I'm gonna stop in Carbondale and keep on going
That Duquesne train gonna ride me night and day

You say I'm a gambler, you say I'm a pimp
But I ain't neither one

Listen to that Duquesne whistle blowin'
Sound like it's on a final run

Listen to that Duquesne whistle blowin'
Blowin' like she never blowed before
Blue light blinkin', red light glowin'
Blowin' like she's at my chamber door

You smiling through the fence at me
Just like you always smiled before

Listen to that Duquesne whistle blowin'
Blowin' like she ain't gonna blow no more

Can't you hear that Duquesne whistle blowin'
Blowin' like the sky's gonna blow apart
You're the only thing alive that keeps me goin'
You're like a time bomb in my heart

I can hear a sweet voice gently calling
Must be the Mother of our Lord

Listen to that Duquesne whistle blowin'
Blowin' like my woman's on board

Listen to that Duquesne whistle blowin'
Blowin' like it's gonna blow my blues away
You ole rascal, I know exactly where you're goin'
I'll lead you there myself at the break of day

I wake up every morning with that woman in my bed
Everybody telling me she's gone to my head

Listen to that Duquesne whistle blowin'
Blowin' like it's gonna kill me dead

Can't you hear that Duquesne whistle blowin'
Blowin' through another no-good town
The lights of my native land are glowin'
I wonder if they'll know me next time around

I wonder if that old oak tree's still standing
That old oak tree, the one we used to climb

Listen to that Duquesne whistle blowin'
Blowin' like she's blowin' right on time

午夜刚过

我搜寻词藻为你唱赞歌
我需要告诉某人
午夜刚过,我的一天才开始

有个名叫宝贝的妞卷走了我的钱
她是个过客
午夜刚过,月亮在我眼中

我兴高采烈,从不胆怯
我待在屠宰间
不赶时间,不怕你动怒
我面对的墙比你面对的更坚固

夏洛特是个娼妓,一袭猩红
玛丽一身绿裳
午夜刚过,我和仙后有个约会

她们叽叽喳喳喋喋不休,这又何妨?
她们躺在自己的血泊里,奄奄一息
脚踩两只船的家伙,有谁听说过他?

我要把他的尸体拖过泥浆

机不可失，时不再来
初遇你时，不觉得你好
午夜刚过，我谁都不要，只要你

Soon After Midnight

I'm searching for phrases to sing your praises
I need to tell someone
It's soon after midnight and my day has just begun

A gal named Honey took my money
She was passing by
It's soon after midnight and the moon is in my eye

My heart is cheerful, it's never fearful
I been down on the killing floors
I'm in no great hurry, I'm not afraid of your fury
I've faced stronger walls than yours

Charlotte's a harlot, dresses in scarlet
Mary dresses in green
It's soon after midnight and I've got a date with a fairy queen

They chirp and they chatter, what does it matter
They're lying there dying in their blood
Two Timing Slim, who's ever heard of him?
I'll drag his corpse through the mud

It's now or never, more than ever
When I met you I didn't think you would do
It's soon after midnight and I don't want nobody but you

窄路

我要穿越沙漠，直到脑子清楚
我甚至不会考虑自己落下了何物
反正那儿没有什么归我所属
回家去，别烦我

这是一条长路，一条又长又窄的路 [1]
如果我追不上你的脚步
那你不妨为我驻足

自从英国人烧毁白宫
市中央便留下一道流血的伤口
我看见你从一个空杯里喝水
我看见你被埋起来又被挖出

这是一条长路，一条又长又窄的路
如果我追不上你的脚步
那你不妨为我驻足

1.《新约·马太福音》7:14："引到永生，那门是窄的，路是小的，找着的人
也少。"

天使从天空俯视

助我疲惫的灵魂升起

我吻你的颊，拉你的犁

你伤了我的心，我不再是你的朋友

这是一条长路，一条又长又窄的路

如果我追不上你的脚步

那你不妨为我驻足

洒着金色阳光的庭院里

你挺身而战或撒腿就溜

你丧失了你可爱的理智

因一杯葡萄酒和一片面包皮

这是一条长路，一条又长又窄的路

如果我追不上你的脚步

那你不妨为我驻足

我们在遥远的海岸大肆掠夺

怎么我那份不如你多？

你父亲离你而去，你母亲也是

连死神都跟你脱离关系

这是一条长路，一条又长又窄的路

如果我追不上你的脚步

那你不妨为我驻足

这个国家里难有活路 [1]

到处是刀刃，划破我的皮肤

我全副武装，努力挣扎

你没法毫发无伤地退走

这是一条长路，一条又长又窄的路

如果我追不上你的脚步

那你不妨为我驻足

你有太多情人在墙边等候

我纵有一千根舌头都数不过来

昨天我本该把他们全扔进大海

今天我连扔一个都够呛

这是一条长路，一条又长又窄的路

如果我追不上你的脚步

那你不妨为我驻足

---

1. 美国西部电影《血战勇士堡》（*Escape from Fort Bravo*, 1953）中的台词。

跳阔步舞的宝贝，你十全十美
用手臂搂着我，那是它们该待的地方
我想带你坐过山车
抚摸你的全身，把你拴在我身旁

这是一条长路，一条又长又窄的路
如果我追不上你的脚步
那你不妨为我驻足

我得到了一个面带微笑的大胸脯女人
她把优雅镶上我的灵魂
我被箭刺破的胸膛还在生疼
我要把头埋进你的乳沟

这是一条长路，一条又长又窄的路
如果我追不上你的脚步
那你不妨为我驻足

晨曦升起，赶走了整夜的漆黑
过去的事情无可挽回
你能守护我安睡
吻走我的眼泪

这是一条长路，一条又长又窄的路
如果我追不上你的脚步
那你不妨为我驻足

我爱女人，她爱男人
我们去过西部又打道回府
黄昏时分，声音响起
"兄弟，温柔点，温柔地祈祝"

这是一条长路，一条又长又窄的路
如果我追不上你的脚步
那你不妨为我驻足

Narrow Way

I'm gonna walk across the desert 'til I'm in my right mind
I won't even think about what I left behind
Nothin' back there anyway I can call my own
Go back home, leave me alone

It's a long road, it's a long and narrow way
If I can't work up to you
You'll have to work down to me someday

Ever since the British burned the white house down
There's a bleeding wound in the heart of town
I saw you drinking from an empty cup
I saw you buried and I saw you dug up

It's a long road, it's a long and narrow way
If I can't work up to you
You'll have to work down to me someday

Look down angel, from the skies
Help my weary soul to rise
I kissed your cheek, I dragged your plow
You broke my heart, I was your friend 'til now

It's a long road, it's a long and narrow way
If I can't work up to you
You'll have to work down to me someday

In the courtyard of the golden sun
You stand and fight or you break and run

You went and lost your lovely head
For a drink of wine and a crust of bread

It's a long road, it's a long and narrow way
If I can't work up to you
You'll have to work down to me someday

We looted and we plundered on distant shores
Why is my share not equal to yours?
Your father left you, your mother too
Even death has washed his hands of you

It's a long road, it's a long and narrow way
If I can't work up to you
You'll have to work down to me someday

This is hard country to stay alive in
Blades are everywhere and they're breaking my skin
I'm armed to the hilt and I'm struggling hard
You won't get out of here unscarred

It's a long road, it's a long and narrow way
If I can't work up to you
You'll have to work down to me someday

You got too many lovers waiting at the wall
If I had a thousand tongues I couldn't count them all
Yesterday I could have thrown them all in the sea
Today, even one may be too much for me

It's a long road, it's a long and narrow way
If I can't work up to you
You'll have to work down to me someday

Cake walking baby, you can do no wrong
Put your arms around me where they belong
I want to take you on a roller coaster ride
Lay my hands all over you, tie you to my side

It's a long road, it's a long and narrow way
If I can't work up to you
You'll have to work down to me someday

I got a heavy stacked woman with a smile on her face
And she has crowned my soul with grace
I'm still hurting from an arrow that pierced my chest
I'm gonna have to take my head and bury it between your
    breasts

It's a long road, it's a long and narrow way
If I can't work up to you
You'll have to work down to me someday

Been dark all night, but now it's dawn
The moving finger is moving on
You can guard me while I sleep
Kiss away the tears I weep

It's a long road, it's a long and narrow way
If I can't work up to you
You'll have to work down to me someday

I love women and she loves men
We've been to the West and we going back again
I heard a voice at the dusk of day
Saying, "Be gentle brother, be gentle and pray"

It's a long road, it's a long and narrow way
If I can't work up to you
You'll have to work down to me someday

蹉跎岁月

已经太久太久
从我们彼此相爱，真心牵手
一度，短暂的一天
我是你的男人

昨晚听到你梦中呓语
说你不该说的话
哦，亲爱的
有一天你会身陷囹圄

我们有处可去？
我们有人可见？
也许适合你的
并不适合我

我二十年没见家人
这不太容易理解
他们可能已经离世
他们失地之后，我就没了他们的消息

摇起来，亲爱的，扭动，尖叫
告诉我这是怎么一回事？
你在太阳底下干吗？
难道不知道太阳会烧坏你大脑？

我的敌人一头撞进地面
我不知道他值多少钱
但他失去了全部，全部乃至更多
他把我当成了多大的蠢货

我戴墨镜遮住眼睛
里面有掩不住的秘密
回来吧，亲爱的
如果我伤害了你的感情，我向你致以歉意

两列火车并肩前行
沿着东线四十英里宽
你不必去，我来找你
因为你是我的伙伴

趁我没看到
身后的整个世界都在燃烧
也许今天，如果不是今天，也许明天

我的悲伤会有个限度

我们在一个霜冻的早晨痛哭
我们因为灵魂被撕裂而痛哭
眼泪就此打住
蹉跎岁月就此止步

Long and Wasted Years

It's been such a long, long time
Since we loved each other and our hearts were true
One time, for one brief day
I was the man for you

Last night I heard you talking in your sleep
Saying things you shouldn't say
Oh, baby
You just might have to go to jail some day

Is there a place we can go?
Is there anybody we can see?
Maybe what's right for you
Isn't really right for me

I ain't seen my family in twenty years
That ain't easy to understand
They may be dead by now
I lost track of them after they lost their land

Shake it up baby, twist and shout
You tell me what it's all about
What you doing out in the sun anyway?
Don't you know the sun can burn your brains right out?

My enemy slammed into the earth
I don't know what he was worth
But he lost it all, everything and more
What a blithering fool he took me for

I wear dark glasses to cover my eyes
There're secrets in them I can't disguise
Come back, baby
If I hurt your feelings, I apologize

Two trains running side by side
Forty miles wide down the Eastern line
You don't have to go, I just came to you
Because you're a friend of mine

I think when my back was turned
The whole world behind me burned
Maybe today, if not today, maybe tomorrow
Maybe there'll be a limit on all my sorrow

We cried on a cold and frosty morn'
We cried because our souls were torn
So much for tears
So much for those long and wasted years

用血支付

哦，我踏踏实实地消磨生命
没什么比我得忍受的更为不幸
我沐浴在太阳的光辉里
能用石头砸死你，因为你犯的那些错

你迟早会犯错
我会给你套上你永远挣不开的枷锁
双腿与双臂，身体与骨头
我用血支付，但不是我自己的

夜复一夜，日复一日
他们揭穿了你无用的希望
我得到越多，给予就越多
我死得越多，活得就越多

我口袋里的东西能让你眼珠子打转
我养的狗能把你撕成几段
我在南方地带的上空盘旋
我用血支付，但不是我自己的

又一个政客用泵抽出他的尿

又一个衣衫褴褛的乞丐抛给你一个飞吻

人生苦短，活不了多久

他们会在早上绞死你，给你唱首歌

一定有人在你酒里下了药

你一饮而尽，然后就发了疯

我的脑袋那么坚硬，一定是用石头做成 [1]

我用血支付，但不是我自己的

我怎么回到家的，无人知晓

我怎么幸免于重重打击的，没人知道

我到地狱走过一遭，这有什么好处？

我问心无愧，你呢？

我会给你主持公道，帮你鼓起钱包

先给我看你的美德

听我呼喊，听我抱怨

我用血支付，但不是我自己的

你在床上咬了你的情人

1.《旧约·以西结书》3:9："我使你的额像金钢钻，比火石更硬。"

过来，我要打破你的烂头

我们的国家必须获得解救和自由

你被指控谋杀，你该如何抗辩？

我就是这样度过光阴

我来埋葬而非赞美 [1]

我会开怀畅饮，独自入睡

我用血支付，但不是我自己的

---

1. 源自莎士比亚的戏剧《裘力斯·凯撒》(*Julius Caesar*) 第三幕第二场：
"我是来埋葬凯撒，不是来赞美他。"（朱生豪译）

Pay in Blood

Well I'm grinding my life away, steady and sure
Nothing more wretched than what I must endure
I'm drenched in the light that shines from the sun
I could stone you to death for the wrongs that you done

Sooner or later you'll make a mistake
I'll put you in a chain that you never can break
Legs and arms and body and bone
I pay in blood, but not my own

Night after night, day after day
They strip your useless hopes away
The more I take, the more I give
The more I die, the more I live

I got something in my pocket make your eyeballs swim
I got dogs that could tear you limb to limb
I'm circling around in the southern zone
I pay in blood, but not my own

Another politician pumping out his piss
Another ragged beggar blowin' ya a kiss
Life is short and it don't last long
They'll hang you in the morning and sing ya a song

Someone must have slipped a drug in your wine
You gulped it down and you lost your mind
My head so hard, it must be made of stone
I pay in blood, but not my own

How I made it back home nobody knows
Or how I survived so many blows
I been through hell, what good did it do?
My conscience is clear, what about you?

I'll give you justice, I'll fatten your purse
Show me your moral virtues first
Hear me holler, hear me moan
I pay in blood but not my own

You bit your lover in the bed
Come here I'll break your lousy head
Our nation must be saved and freed
You been accused of murder, how do you plead?

This is how I spend my days
I came to bury not to praise
I'll drink my fill and sleep alone
I pay in blood, but not my own

猩红镇

在我的出生地猩红镇
有常春藤叶和银色荆刺
你不会念那些街道的名字
黄金只剩下四分之一盎司

音乐响起，人们缓缓摆动
他们都在问，我们是一路人？
汤姆叔叔还在为比尔叔叔打工
猩红镇在山脚下

五月里的猩红镇
亲爱的威廉躺在临终床上
玛丽小姐守在床边
亲吻他的脸，祈祷上苍

他那么勇敢那么温柔那么忠诚
我会为他流泪，就像他也会为我流泪
蓝衣小男孩，来吹你的小号
在我的出生地猩红镇

炎热正午里的猩红镇

有棕榈叶的影子和零星的鲜花

乞丐蹲在门下

救助来了，但来得太迟

大理石板上，石头地里

你把你卑微的心愿告诉我们

我摸摸衣服，褶边已有裂缝

在我的出生地猩红镇

猩红镇里，末日将临

七大奇观都在这里

善与恶并肩共存

所有人形荣耀加身

把你的心放进大盘子，看谁会来咬

看谁会抱着你，吻你说晚安

猩红镇里有枫树林和胡桃园

哭泣于你何益

猩红镇里，你与你父亲的仇敌交战

山岗之上，寒风劲吹

你和他们在高处打，和他们在低处干

你用威士忌、吗啡和杜松子酒壮胆

你的大腿能让男人疯狂
很多我希望我们做的事却没有做
猩红镇里，天空晴朗
你真希望自己就待在这里

上几杯酒，乔，来一曲《踱来踱去》
为我平胸的吸毒妓女
我在熬夜，将功补过
当天堂的微笑骤然笼罩

如果爱是罪孽，那美就是犯罪
一切风华正茂时都很美
黑人、白人、黄人和棕人
猩红镇里你都会遇到

Scarlet Town

In Scarlet Town where I was born
There's ivy leaf and silver thorn
The streets have names you can't pronounce
Gold is down to a quarter of an ounce

The music starts and the people sway
Everybody says, are you going my way?
Uncle Tom still working for Uncle Bill
Scarlet Town is under the hill

Scarlet Town in the month of May
Sweet William on his deathbed lay
Mistress Mary by the side of the bed
Kissing his face, heaping prayers on his head

So brave, so true, so gentle is he
I'll weep for him as he'd weep for me
Little Boy Blue come blow your horn
In Scarlet Town where I was born

Scarlet Town in the hot noon hours
There's palm leaf shadows and scattered flowers
Beggars crouching at the gate
Help comes but it comes too late

On marble slabs and in fields of stone
You make your humble wishes known
I touched the garment but the hem was torn
In Scarlet Town where I was born

In Scarlet Town the end is near
The seven wonders of the world are here
The evil and the good living side by side
All human forms seem glorified

Put your heart on a platter and see who'll bite
See who'll hold you and kiss you good night
There's walnut groves and maple wood
In Scarlet Town crying won't do you no good

In Scarlet Town you fight your father's foes
Up on the hill a chilly wind blows
You fight 'em on high and you fight 'em down in
You fight 'em with whisky, morphine and gin

You got legs that can drive men mad
A lot of things we didn't do that I wish we had
In Scarlet Town the sky is clear
You'll wish to God that you stayed right here

Set 'em up Joe, play Walking The Floor
Play it for my flat chested junkie whore
I'm staying up late and I'm making amends
While the smile of heaven descends

If love is a sin then beauty is a crime
All things are beautiful in their time
The black and the white, the yellow and the brown
It's all right there for ya in Scarlet Town

古罗马国王 [1]

那些古罗马国王，一身鲨皮呢西装

蝴蝶领结、金属徽章和高帮靴

打入道钉，开道筑路

头戴高礼帽，身穿燕尾服，被钉进棺木

飞走吧，小鸟，飞走，扇动你的翅膀

趁着夜色远走高飞，像古罗马国王一样

那些古罗马国王，一大早

下山分发玉米

树林中飞驰，铁路上疾驶

你试图逃跑，被他们拽回来

明天是周五，不知道明天会怎样

人人都在议论古罗马国王

他们是毒贩，四处插手，买进卖出

他们摧毁你的城市，也摧毁你

他们好色奸诈，不择手段

每个人都比你们加起来更壮

---

1. 罗马国王，20 世纪六七十年代美国纽约的一个帮派组织。

重拳手和抢劫犯戴着花哨的金戒指

所有女人都为古罗马国王疯狂

我用凝着血块的布修饰你的伤口

我不怕和小泼妇或老丑婆做爱

如果你站在那儿，看到我过来

就在空中挥挥你的手帕

我还没有死，我的铃还在响

我十指交叉，像古罗马国王一样

我会剥夺你的生命，剥夺你的呼吸

把你运进死亡之屋

有一天你会找我聊天

除了我你谁都不想见

把我的小提琴拿来，把弦调准

我要疯狂奏响，像古罗马国王一样[1]

底特律沦陷那天我在黑山上

他们斩尽杀绝，送他们进地狱

---

1. 传说尼禄火烧罗马城时弹着竖琴伴奏。

叮咚老爸[1]，你没达到期望

我要把你送上西西里法庭

我快活过，风流过

我要把他们的钱骗光，像古罗马国王一样

---

1. 20 世纪 40 年代，美国旧金山城市铁路电车售票员弗兰西斯·范·威（Francis Van Wie）坐拥十八个妻子，犯了重婚罪，当时有首歌叫作《我是来自杜马斯的叮咚老爸》(I'm a Ding Dong Daddy from Dumas)，媒体便戏称其为"叮咚老爸"；美国动画片《少年泰坦》(Teen Titans) 中有一人物也叫"叮咚老爸"。

Early Roman Kings

All the early Roman Kings in their sharkskin suits
Bowties and buttons, high top boots
Driving the spikes in, blazing the rails
Nailed in their coffins in top hats and tails
Fly away little bird, fly away, flap your wings
Fly by night like the early Roman Kings

All the early Roman Kings in the early, early morn'
Coming down the mountain, distributing the corn
Speeding through the forest, racing down the track
You try to get away, they drag you back
Tomorrow is Friday, we'll see what it brings
Everybody's talking 'bout the early Roman Kings

They're peddlers and they're meddlers, they buy and they
  sell
They destroyed your city, they'll destroy you as well
They're lecherous and treacherous, hell bent for leather
Each of them bigger than all men put together
Sluggers and muggers wearing fancy gold rings
All the women going crazy for the early Roman Kings

I'll dress up your wounds with a blood clotted rag
I ain't afraid to make love to a bitch or a hag
If you see me coming and you're standing there
Wave your handkerchief in the air
I ain't dead yet, my bell still rings
I keep my fingers crossed like the early Roman Kings

I'll strip you of life, strip you of breath
Ship you down to the house of death
One day you will ask for me
There'll be no one else that you'll want to see
Bring down my fiddle, tune up my strings
Gonna break it wide open like the early Roman Kings

I was up on black mountain the day Detroit fell
They killed them all off and they sent them to hell
Ding Dong Daddy, you're coming up short
Gonna put you on trial in a Sicilian court
I've had my fun, I've had my flings
Gonna shake 'em all down like the early Roman Kings

锡天使

昨晚主人回来晚了
回到他空寂的宅邸和落寞的王座
仆人对他说："主人，夫人走了
天将破晓时走的。"

"有话你就说吧，说吧，伙计，
尽可能地直说。"
"老亨利·李，部落首领，
骑马穿过树林，拉着她的手。"

主人平躺在床上
诅咒着高温，抱紧着脑袋
深思着自己的未来
再等一天将为时太晚

"把我的外套和领带拿来
还有最便宜的劳力
给我的鹿皮色母马备好鞍
如果你看到我经过，给我做个祈祷。"

哦，他们骑了一夜又一天
一路向东，沿着大公路
他心神倦怠，视线模糊
他的伙计们弃他而去，而他继续向前

他来到一个昏暗之地
前额锤击般的疼
心如刀绞般的痛
失眠在脑海里蔓延

哦，他扔掉头盔和十字手柄宝剑
宣布放弃他的信念，否定他的上帝
他匍匐前进，把耳朵贴在墙上
不管怎样，他要做个了结

他弯腰割断电线
盯着火焰，哼着怒火
黑暗中瞥见两人
很难确定谁是谁

他用金链条把自己放下来
每根静脉里的神经都在哆嗦
每个指关节都在流血，他深吸一口气

用手指理了理油腻的头发

他俩彼此对视，玻璃杯碰得叮当响
像个不可分割的整体
"有种奇怪的预感，有个男人就在附近。"
"不用担心，他连只苍蝇都不忍心杀。"

主人从帘子后面走进屋
向前移步，拴上屋门
阴影遮住了他的皱纹
和古老宗族的所有尊贵

她转过身，一脸错愕的神情
还有冲天的憎恶
"你是个鲁莽的蠢货，从你眼里看得出。
你跑来绝非明智之举。"

"起来，站起来，你这贪婪的少妇
把脸捂起来，不然后果自负。
你让我感到恶心，
赶紧穿上衣服。"

"傻小子，以为我是圣女，

不想再听你抱怨。

你只给了我最甜蜜的谎言。

给我住口，看着就好。"

"我本会送你星星和星球

但这些东西于你何益？

膝盖不屈下可以，心得屈下

否则你再也见不到这世界。"

"噢，请别那么冷酷，

我爱他胜过爱黄金。"

"噢，亲爱的，你一定瞎了眼。

他是个没胆又没脑的猩猩。"

"一直都是我顺着你，

现在该由我来决断。

想跑，"他咒骂道

"先过了我这关。"

"不要冲动行事，

你以为我很蠢。

先生，你不能否认

你让我出了大洋相，这是为什么？"

"不会再接这无礼的话茬，

魔鬼会带你走，我拭目以待。

赶快给我让开，

不想早死的话。"

枪声砰然响起，清脆无比

第一枪擦过耳朵

第二枪正中目标

他像个扭弯的别针一样弯了下去

他爬到屋角，垂下头

紧握椅子，抓住床

针和线已无法补缝他的伤口

血从嘴里冒出来，他大限已到

"你这个魔鬼，你杀了我老公。"

"老公？什么老公？你到底什么意思？

他是个惹是生非的罪人。

我杀掉他，准备把他抛进风中。"

"听着，"她气呼呼地说，

"你也应该去见死神。

是我拯救了你的灵魂。"

她掀起睡袍，拔出一把刀

他一脸僵硬，满面汗水
臂膀酸痛，手心湿透
"你是凶残王后，嗜血人妻。
把刀递给我，如果你不介意。"

"我俩很相像，血都滚烫，
但身体和想法一点也不像。
所有丈夫都是好男人，所有妻子都知道。"
她刺向他的心脏，鲜血流淌

他膝盖一软，伸手抓门
他在劫难逃，滑落地板
他在她耳边低声说："全是你的错，
我的战斗生涯就此停顿。"

她摸摸他的嘴唇，亲吻他的脸颊
他想说话，但已气息奄奄
"你为我而死，现在我要为你而死。"
她刺向她的心脏，一刀刺穿

三个情人堆成一团

抛进墓里永远安眠

葬礼火把熊熊燃烧

燃亮市镇村庄，整夜整天

Tin Angel

It was late last night when the boss came home
To a deserted mansion and a desolate throne
Servant said, "Boss, the lady's gone
She left this morning just 'fore dawn."

"You got something to tell me, tell it to me, man.
Come to the point as straight as you can."
"Old Henry Lee, chief of the clan,
Came riding through the woods and took her by the hand."

The boss he laid back flat on his bed
He cursed the heat and he clutched his head
He pondered the future of his fate
To wait another day would be far too late

"Go fetch me my coat and my tie
And the cheapest labor that money can buy
Saddle me up my buckskin mare
If you see me go by, put up a prayer."

Well, they rode all night and they rode all day
Eastward long on the broad highway
His spirit was tired and his vision was bent
His men deserted him and onward he went

He came to a place where the light was dull
His forehead pounding in his skull
Heavy heart was wracked with pain
Insomnia raging in his brain

Well he threw down his helmet and his cross-handled sword
He renounced his faith, he denied his Lord
Crawled on his belly, put his ear to the wall
One way or another he'd put an end to it all

He leaned down, cut the electric wire
Stared into the flames and he snorted the fire
Peered through the darkness, caught a glimpse of the two
It was hard to tell for certain who was who

He lowered himself down on a golden chain
His nerves were quaking in every vein
His knuckles were bloody, he sucked in the air
He ran his fingers through his greasy hair

They looked at each other and their glasses clinked
One single unit inseparably linked
"Got a strange premonition there's a man close by."
"Don't worry about him, he wouldn't harm a fly."

From behind the curtain the boss crossed the floor
He moved his feet and he bolted the door
Shadows hiding the lines in his face
With all the nobility of an ancient race

She turned, she was startled with a look of surprise
With a hatred that could hit the skies
"You're a reckless fool, I can see it in your eyes.
To come this way was by no means wise."

"Get up, stand up, you greedy lipped wench
And cover your face or suffer the consequence.
You are making my heart full sick.

Put your clothes back on double quick."

"Silly boy, you think me a saint.
I'll listen no more to your words of complaint.
You've given me nothing but the sweetest lies.
Now hold your tongue and feed your eyes."

"I'd have given you the stars and the planets too
But what good would these things do you?
Bow the heart, if not the knee
Or never again this world you'll see."

"Oh, please let not your heart be cold.
This man is dearer to me than gold."
"Oh my dear, you must be blind.
He's a gutless ape with a worthless mind."

"You had your way too long with me.
Now it's me who'll determine how things shall be.
Try to escape," he cussed and cursed
"You'll have to try to get past me first."

"I dare not let your passion rule.
You think my heart, the heart of a fool.
And you sir, you cannot deny
You made a monkey of me, what and for why?"

"I'll have no more of this insulting chat.
The devil can have you, I'll see to that.
Look sharp or step aside,
Or in the cradle you'll wish you died."

The gun went boom and the shot rang clear

First bullet grazed his ear
Second ball went right straight in
And he bent in the middle like a twisted pin

He crawled to the corner and he lowered his head
He gripped the chair and he grabbed the bed
It would take more than needle and thread
Bleeding from the mouth, he's as good as dead

"You shot my husband down, you fiend."
"Husband, what husband, what the hell do you mean?
He was a man of strife, a man of sin.
I cut him down and I'll throw him to the wind."

"Hear this," she said, with angry breath
"You too shall meet the lord of death.
It was I who brought your soul to life."
And she raised her robe and she drew out a knife

His face was hard and caked with sweat
His arms ached and his hands were wet
"You're a murderous queen and a bloody wife.
If you don't mind, I'll have the knife."

"We're two of a kind and our blood runs hot.
But we're no way similar in body and thought.
All husbands are good men, as all wives know."
Then she pierced him to the heart and his blood did flow

His knees went limp and he reached for the door
His doom was sealed, he slid to the floor
He whispered in her ear, "This is all your fault.
My fighting days have come to a halt."

She touched his lip and kissed his cheek
He tried to speak, but his breath was weak
"You died for me, now I'll die for you."
She put the blade to her heart and she ran it through

All three lovers together in a heap
Thrown into the grave forever to sleep
Funeral torches blazed away
Through the towns and the villages all night and all day

暴风雨

苍白的月亮壮丽地升起
在西部的小镇
她诉说着一个悲伤的故事
关于那艘沉没的巨轮

那是四月十四日
她在海浪里航行
航向未来
航向预言中的黄金时代

星光映亮了夜晚
大海清晰可见
穿过那些阴影
约定的时辰已近

灯光四平八稳
掠过泛起的白沫
所有的贵族与淑女
航向永恒的家园

枝形吊灯开始摇晃

在栏杆的上方

管弦乐队正在演奏

凋谢的爱情之歌

守夜人躺在睡梦中

伴着舞厅里舞者的转动

他梦到泰坦尼克号正在下沉

沉入地下世界

利奥拿起他的素描本 [1]

他老想画上几笔

他闭上眼睛画下

他脑海里的风景

丘比特射中了他的心

啪的一声射穿了它

离他最近的女人

他跌倒进她的怀抱

---

1. 泰坦尼克号罹难者中有一位德国农民利奥·齐默曼（Leo Zimmermann），
迪伦本姓齐默曼（Zimmerman）；又，电影中美国演员莱昂纳多·迪卡普里
奥（Leonardo DiCaprio）饰演的男主角曾为女主角画素描。

他听到高声喧嚣

听起来很不对劲

他的内心告诉他

此地不宜久留

他踉跄着走上后甲板

现在可没时间睡觉

后甲板上的积水

已经深达三尺

烟囱倒向一边

沉重的脚步咚咚作响

他走进一片纷乱

四周天旋地转

船在沉没

宇宙张开大口

上帝念着进天堂的名单

天使别过头

走廊里的灯光

昏暗模糊地摇曳

死尸已经浮起

在双层底的船体

引擎接着爆炸
螺旋桨无法动弹
锅炉不堪重负
船头分崩离析

乘客被甩得飞起
向后向前，又快又远
他们嘟哝着，摸索着，跌撞着
一个比一个疲倦

面纱被撕得粉碎
在十二点和一点之间
没有改变，没有奇迹
来将覆水收回

守夜人躺在睡梦中
倾斜成四十五度角
他梦到泰坦尼克号正在下沉
沉到她的膝下

惠灵顿正在睡觉

床铺开始滑动

他勇敢的心在跳动

他把桌子推到一旁

破碎的水晶玻璃

洒了一地

他把两把手枪绑在身上

他还能坚持多久？

他的手下和同伴

已不见影踪

他在寂静中等候

时间和空间插手

狭窄的过道

黑暗的天空

他看到各种悲痛

听到四处呼号

警铃鸣响

想阻挡汹涌的浪潮

友人们和恋人们

紧紧依偎彼此依靠

母亲和她们的女儿

走下楼梯

跳进冰冷的海水

爱和怜悯送走了她们的祷告

那个有钱人埃斯特先生

亲吻了他的爱妻

他无从知晓

这是这辈子最后一趟旅程

卡尔文、布莱克和威尔逊

在黑暗中打赌

他们没一个能活下来

讲述上岸的故事

兄弟同室操戈

任何境遇之下

他们互相残杀

跳着死亡之舞

他们从沉没的船上

放下救生艇

那里有变节者和叛徒

摔断的腰和摔断的颈

主教离开客舱
来帮助需要帮助的人
他仰望天堂
说："这些穷人归您来养。"

那个妓院老板戴维
出来遣散了他的姑娘们
他看到水越来越深
他的世界正在变更

吉姆·丹迪面含微笑
他从没学过游泳
他看到一个跛脚的孩童
就把座位让给了他

他看到星光闪耀
从东方照来
死神暴跳如雷
但他心若止水

他们封住舱口

但舱门顶不住
他们溺毙身亡
在黄铜镀金楼梯上

利奥对克利奥说
"我想我快疯了。"
他已经失去了心智
不管他有什么样的心智

他努力堵住门口
让大家免受伤害
血从伤口涌出
顺着胳膊倾注

花瓣纷纷落下
直到一片不剩
时间漫长而可怕
巫师的诅咒还在应验

主人在倒白兰地
他慢慢沉入海里
他坚守到最后
最后一个走

还有好多、好多人

在这儿默默无闻，直至永远

他们从未驶上海洋

从未离开家乡

守夜人躺在睡梦中

灾难已经铸成

他梦到泰坦尼克号正在下沉

他试图告知别人

船长难以呼吸

跪在舵轮旁

在他上方和下方

是五万吨的钢

他看了看罗盘

凝视着它的表面

指针指向下方

他明白他已经败北

昏暗的光亮里

他回忆起过去的年岁

他读过《启示录》

将杯中填满泪水

当死神的任务完成
一千六百人已经安息
好人、坏人、富人和穷人
最可爱的和最优秀的

他们在岸上等待
他们试图弄明白
但没什么可弄明白的
一切都在上帝手中

电报传来消息
多么致命的打击
爱失去了激情
一切听其自然

守夜人躺在睡梦中
梦着一切可能
他梦到泰坦尼克号正在下沉
沉入深蓝色的海底

Tempest

The pale moon rose in its glory
Out on the western town
She told a sad, sad story
Of the great ship that went down

'Twas the fourteen day of April
Over the waves she rode
Sailing into tomorrow
To a golden age foretold

The night was bright with starlight
The seas were sharp and clear
Moving through the shadows
The promised hour was near

Lights were holding steady
Gliding over the foam
All the lords and ladies
Heading for their eternal home

The chandeliers were swaying
From the balustrades above
The orchestra was playing
Songs of faded love

The watchman he lay dreaming
As the ballroom dancers twirled
He dreamed the Titanic was sinking
Into the underworld

Leo took his sketchbook
He was often so inclined
He closed his eyes and painted
The scenery in his mind

Cupid struck his bosom
And broke it with a snap
The closest woman to him
He fell into her lap

He heard a loud commotion
Something sounded wrong
His inner spirit was saying
That he couldn't stand here long

He staggered to the quarterdeck
No time now to sleep
Water on the quarterdeck
Already three foot deep

Smokestack leaning sideways
Heavy feet began to pound
He walked into the whirlwind
Sky spinning all around

The ship was going under
The universe opened wide
The roll was called up yonder
The angels turned aside

Lights down in the hallway
Flickering dim and dull
Dead bodies already floating

In the double bottomed hull

The engines then exploded
Propellers they failed to start
The boilers overloaded
The ship's bow split apart

Passengers were flying
Backward, forward, far and fast
They mumbled, fumbled, tumbled
Each one more weary than the last

The veil was torn asunder
'Tween the hours of twelve and one
No change, no sudden wonder
Could undo what had been done

The watchman lay there dreaming
At forty-five degrees
He dreamed the Titanic was sinking
Dropping to her knees

Wellington, he was sleeping
His bed began to slide
His valiant heart was beating
He pushed the tables aside

Glass of shattered crystal
Lay scattered 'round about
He strapped on both his pistols
How long could he hold out?

His men and his companions

Were nowhere to be seen
In silence there he waited for
Time and space to intervene

The passageway was narrow
There was blackness in the air
He saw every kind of sorrow
Heard voices everywhere

Alarm bells were ringing
To hold back the swelling tide
Friends and lovers clinging
To each other side by side

Mothers and their daughters
Descending down the stairs
Jumped into the icy waters
Love and pity sent their prayers

The rich man, Mr. Astor
Kissed his darling wife
He had no way of knowing
Be the last trip of his life

Calvin, Blake and Wilson
Gambled in the dark
Not one of them would ever live to
Tell the tale of disembark

Brother rose up against brother
In every circumstance
They fought and slaughtered each other
In a deadly dance

They lowered down the lifeboats
From the sinking wreck
There were traitors, there were turncoats
Broken backs and broken necks

The bishop left his cabin
To help all those in need
Turned his eyes up to the heavens
Said, "The poor are yours to feed."

Davey the brothel keeper
Came out, dismissed his girls
Saw the water getting deeper
Saw the changing of his world

Jim Dandy smiled
He'd never learned to swim
Saw the little crippled child
And he gave his seat to him

He saw the starlight shining
Streaming from the East
Death was on the rampage
But his heart was now at peace

They battened down the hatches
But the hatches wouldn't hold
They drowned upon the staircase
Of brass and polished gold

Leo said to Cleo
"I think I'm going mad."
But he'd lost his mind already

Whatever mind he had

He tried to block the doorway
To save all those from harm
Blood from an open wound
Pouring down his arm

Petals fell from flowers
'Til all of them were gone
In the long and dreadful hours
The wizard's curse played on

The host was pouring brandy
He was going down slow
He stayed right 'til the end
He was the last to go

There were many, many others
Nameless here forevermore
They'd never sailed the ocean
Or left their homes before

The watchman, he lay dreaming
The damage had been done
He dreamed the Titanic was sinking
And he tried to tell someone

The captain, barely breathing
Kneeling at the wheel
Above him and beneath him
Fifty thousand tons of steel

He looked over at his compass

And he gazed into its face
Needle pointing downward
He knew he lost the race

In the dark illumination
He remembered bygone years
He read the Book of Revelation
And he filled his cup with tears

When the Reaper's task had ended
Sixteen hundred had gone to rest
The good, the bad, the rich, the poor
The loveliest and the best

They waited at the landing
And they tried to understand
But there is no understanding
On the judgment of God's hand

News came over the wires
And struck with deadly force
Love had lost its fires
All things had run their course

The watchman he lay dreaming
Of all things that can be
He dreamed the Titanic was sinking
Into the deep blue sea

前进吧，约翰

医生，医生，告诉我时间
又喝掉一瓶酒，又花掉一便士
他转过身，缓慢离去
他们从他背后开枪，他倒下

闪耀你的光芒
继续前进
你燃烧得如此绚烂
前进吧，约翰

从利物浦的码头到汉堡的红灯区
到采石场和采石工在一起
为人山人海演，为便宜座位演
你生命中的又一天，去往你旅程的终点

闪耀你的光芒
继续前进
你燃烧得如此绚烂
前进吧，约翰

乘着向南吹的信风航行
身上破衣烂衫，就像其他奴隶
他们绑住你的手，封住你的嘴
没法子走出这又深又暗的洞穴

闪耀你的光芒
继续前进
你燃烧得如此绚烂
前进吧，约翰

我今日听到这新闻，我的天
他们把你的船拖到了岸边
如今城市漆黑一片，不再有欢颜
人们撕裂般心痛，痛到最深处

闪耀你的光芒
继续前进
你燃烧得如此绚烂
前进吧，约翰

放下你的包，将行李收拾好
现在就走，差不多没错
走得越早，回来得越快

你被禁锢在这座岛上太久太久

闪耀你的光芒
继续前进
你燃烧得如此绚烂
前进吧，约翰

慢些走，你走得太快
立刻一起到我这儿来
你筋骨疲惫，还剩一口气
老天，你知道这有多难

闪耀你的光芒
继续前进
你燃烧得如此绚烂
前进吧，约翰

前进吧，约翰，迎着雨雪前进
走右边那条路，到水牛的徜徉地
他们设套伏击，在你知道之前
现在想回家为时已晚

闪耀你的光芒

继续前进

你燃烧得如此绚烂

前进吧，约翰

老虎，老虎，灼灼燃亮

求主守护我的灵魂

在黑夜的森林里 [1]

遮住他，让他安息

闪耀你的光芒

继续前进

你燃烧得如此绚烂

前进吧，约翰

---

1. 此节第一、三行歌词引用威廉·布莱克的诗歌《老虎》(The Tyger)。

Roll on John

Doctor, doctor, tell me the time of day
Another bottle's empty, another penny spent
He turned around and he slowly walked away
They shot him in the back and down he went

Shine your light
Move it on
You burned so bright
Roll on, John

From the Liverpool docks to the red light Hamburg streets
Down in the quarry with the Quarrymen
Playing to the big crowds, playing to the cheap seats
Another day in the life on your way to your journey's end

Shine your light
Move it on
You burned so bright
Roll on, John

Sailing through the trade winds bound for the South
Rags on your back just like any other slave
They tied your hands and they clamped your mouth
Wasn't no way out of that deep, dark cave

Shine your light
Move it on
You burned so bright
Roll on, John

I heard the news today, oh boy
They hauled your ship up on the shore
Now the city gone dark, there is no more joy
They tore the heart right out and cut it to the core

Shine your light
Move it on
You burned so bright
Roll on, John

Put down your bags and get 'em packed
Leave right now, you won't be far from wrong
The sooner you go, the quicker you'll be back
You been cooped up on an island far too long

Shine your light
Move it on
You burned so bright
Roll on, John

Slow down, you're moving way too fast
Come together right now over me
Your bones are weary, you're about to breathe your last
Lord, you know how hard that it can be

Shine your light
Move it on
You burned so bright
Roll on, John

Roll on John, roll through the rain and snow
Take the right hand road and go where the buffalo roam
They'll trap you in an ambush 'fore you know

Too late now to sail back home

Shine your light
Move it on
You burned so bright
Roll on, John

Tyger, tyger, burning bright
I pray the Lord my soul to keep
In the forest of the night
Cover him over, and let him sleep

Shine your light
Move it on
You burned so bright
Roll on, John